HIGH PRICED SILENCE

Oh, The Secrets We Keep

TJ Thomas

Heart 2 Pen Creatives, LLC

DEDICATION

In the loving memory of my mom,
the late Amy Douthit (Mitchell)

◆

Mom, Thank you for being my biggest supporter, the most remarkable example of strength, my biggest fan, and especially for being the live and in-color representation of a survivor.

ACKNOWLEDGMENTS

To my husband, Allan, thank you for your unwavering support, encouragement, and love.

To Heart 2 Pen Creatives, thank you isn't enough to express my sincere appreciation for your guidance and support in bringing my story to life.

To those who buy, gift, or read this book,
Thank you.

TABLE OF *Contents*

INTRODUCTION

W hat doesn't kill you makes you stronger…at least that's what they say! We've all heard it before; Kelly Clarkson even wrote a song about it. It's what we tell ourselves in times of tribulation, hoping it will instantly heal our wounds. It's also the "words of wisdom," usually from a friend or family member with the best intentions, given when the message is too difficult to receive. This widely used "mantra" suggests that if one does not break physically, spiritually, or mentally during a storm of chaos, then the experience should be recognized as part of the grooming process…a process that provides preparation for whatever new "pitfall" awaits.

That sounds good in theory, but I'm sure it didn't take *this* situation into account…how could it have? To say I am in disbelief is an understatement. Tears are flooding my eyes. My screams are going unheard. As I looked down from the 15th floor, visions of my life (past, present, and future) flashed before me like a silent movie. With blood rushing to my head, the realization that I'm hanging headfirst to what is sure to be my death becomes more apparent by the second. NONE of my life experiences, up to this very moment, have equipped me for this. There was no grooming. Even the most famed Hollywood writers couldn't have developed a saga of this magnitude. How in the world am I supposed to be strong while being dangled from the side of a building? Here's an FYI...I AM NOT STRONG...I AM ABOUT TO FALL TO MY DEATH!!!

All that is left for me to do is pray. Dear God...

$\mathcal{N\!ot}$ TODAY SATAN

B ut let's go back…

May 1999…you know, the year Prince made famous…and if you were a purple paisley-wearing, Prince fanatic like me, you were fully prepared for the year to be a hit, just like the song. Well, it lived up to the hype in some areas, but in others…it missed the mark.

It was the last week of the spring semester; the last seven days of my junior year in college. However, because I had completed all my exams, it was already official…I was A COLLEGE SENIOR! I finally made it to this coveted year: the year of academic distinction, the year that people say would make or break you. But I wasn't scared. "Move out of the way world, and let me at it," was my thought process. This was a dream that I'd been waiting for forever. It was like waiting for the double-dutch rope to line up just right so you could jump in and show everyone whatcha got. It was MY time…or so I thought.

There was plenty of movement on campus, as the start

of the first semester and the end of the Spring semester were always the busiest. Some students were packing to head home, some were finishing exams, and others were just hanging around with nowhere to go and nothing to do. In my mind, Summer had begun for me. I was the newest member of the Class of 2000, and after a long few months, I was so looking forward to going home to see my family. But first, I had to pay a visit to my advisor. Although I was confident that I had done everything required of me, I didn't want to be complacent and assume anything. I had to be 100% sure that nothing had changed since my last degree audit before the Spring semester. It is no secret among some HBCU students that at any given time, ridiculousness and trickery could pop up out of nowhere and shut the power off on your dreams without notice. I refuse to let that be the case for me. I stayed proactive and aware, so there were no questions about my educational status at the end of the day.

What was expected to be a great meeting with my advisor was the complete opposite. I remember it like it was yesterday. After finishing one of the most challenging years in my academic career and finally feeling like I could see the light at the end of this very long tunnel, the unthinkable began unfolding right before my eyes. Sitting on the edge of the seat across from my advisor's desk, I could tell something was not quite right. I don't know…call it intuition, or spider senses, or call it, "I could feel it in my spirit." Whatever it was, I knew in my gut that this very casual and routine meeting would be anything but routine. The sound of her flipping through my paperwork was the only thing drowning out the awkward silence in the room. Eventually, she looked up, with little to no expression, and advised me that the department in charge of my program major was in jeopardy of losing its accreditation. Without waiting for my response (even though I was speechless), she quickly continued explaining that I could still proceed with the major, but they could not guarantee the program would meet the required standards by graduation. In other words, even if I complete the remaining classes, without the accreditation, my degree would be invalid. Wait…what the what!?!

I could feel my pressure rising and my head spinning in an instant. As the first of my parents' kids to graduate from college, I could think of nothing else at that moment except my plans…my goals…my dreams… all of my hard work…the sacrifices I made this past year…the long nights spent writing papers, the overwhelming stress, and the never-ending tears. I had become a social hermit, for crying out loud, to bring my

GPA back up from what I refer to as my "I DID IT" BIG Sophomore Debacle! I had to fix what I broke.

Unlike most, I aced my freshman year and made the Dean's list. However, the second time around, I was not so triumphant. I figured that since I did well as a freshman, as a sophomore, it was a no-brainer. LIES, I tell ya! ALL LIES! Don't get me wrong, I was an overachiever at everything in my life (up to this point). In this case, I succeeded at partying and having a ball, and especially at academic destruction! Like dominoes, I could see the pieces falling but couldn't stop them. This was on me, though, which is why I worked so hard to get back on track. So, WHAT ABOUT THIS BEING MY TIME DOES SHE NOT UNDERSTAND!?!?! What am I supposed to do with this information? As I tried to collect my thoughts and regain my composure, I began going through a plethora of emotions in a matter of seconds. At first, I felt such despair, as if my plane had crashed on a deserted island and I was the lone survivor. Then it quickly turned to the feeling of defeat; you know that gut-wrenching feeling when you watch that three-point shot go in, all-net, as the clock runs out and ends what should have been your championship season. But before I could process that feeling, it had already turned into anger... that "BURN IT DOWN" anger. That "Angela Bassett, Waiting to Exhale, toss the match and walk away" anger. I literally saw red and felt that the only viable solution to the problem THEY had created was to burn this mutha' TO! THE! GROUND! It may seem a bit irrational now, but nothing about my thinking could be confused with rational. I even called my mom to give her a heads up on my plans to set this school ablaze before she saw her baby on the 11:00 news later that night.

I was inconsolable. I was at a crossroads in my collegiate career and had no idea what to do or which path to take. Only thirty minutes earlier, I was nine credit hours from graduation. Now, someone was telling me that the years I spent working towards this English degree were in jeopardy of meaning nothing. To make matters worse, I had to complete 36 hours to graduate by May 2000.

Under any other circumstances, I would have started formulating a new plan as soon as I finished breaking things to release my frustration. However, this was different. I needed guidance, and the one person I thought could point me in the right direction had seemingly already given up on me and wasn't interested in helping any further. But as my advisor, this was her job, and I didn't know what else to do, so I reluctantly asked her one last question…What are my options? Her tone, her attitude, and the smirk on her face spoke volumes as she added one last nail to my coffin. She picked up my transcripts, walked closer, and leaned toward me as if sharing a secret. Then, in the most condescending way possible, she said that graduating with my class was not going to happen but that I could change majors and maybe graduate next year, 2001. However, it was a long shot and most likely not going to happen because of the particular courses I needed, the times they were being held, and how they were structured. And oh yeah, let's not forget that I had already missed the enrollment deadline to start the summer semester. That was the cherry on top of this quickly melting sundae.

Enough was enough. I had heard all I could bear to hear. It was time for me to put on my big girl pants and figure it out because it was apparent that no one else was going to. Desperation replaced anger, and I immediately jumped into survival mode. Though my resources were limited, I knew that whatever course of action I needed to take from this point on would not include starting over. It had to keep me on track to graduate on time. This was going to work...it had to work...there was no other option.

I felt as if I was having Deja Vu. I had been here before. Though the circumstances were different, the heartbreak felt the same. Three years earlier, the plans I had for my freshman semester were derailed after a devasting sports injury. I had worked my butt off and earned a track scholarship that took some of the financial burdens off of my mom. Unfortunately, I suffered a traumatic hip dislocation that ended my track career in the blink of an eye. My spot on the team was gone, along with my scholarship. This was a big blow to my carefully thought-out plan, but I would not be denied.

For as long as I can remember, my goal was to become a lawyer. I was never short on determination, so no matter what came my way, I was hell-bent on making that dream a reality. With that being said, it was time to enact Plan B because tuition wasn't going to pay itself. Thankfully, I had my academic scholarship to fall back on. However, I still had to work a full-time job while juggling a full course load in order to cover the tuition cost that was lacking.

As I left the advisor's office, all the feelings of that tumultuous time came rushing back. I didn't know how I would do it, but I knew it was graduation or bust.

2

A *Ram* IN THE BUSH

I stood in the lobby, dazed and depleted, as if I had just gone 10 rounds with Tyson. Suddenly, my legs began to feel weak, and I needed to sit down. When I reached the nearest bench, my body went limp; I dropped down onto the cushioned seat and began to cry. How could this be happening to me? I have worked so hard! I don't deserve this!! These are the thoughts that I wanted to scream out at the top of my lungs in the middle of the busy lobby, but I held them in. The flood of tears said it all. Graduating on time meant more than anything to me because it would mark the beginning of what I had laid out for my future. However, reality stared me in the face, and I felt as if I was stuck in quicksand and sinking at an alarming rate.

I needed to pull it together. This was only a minor setback…at least that was what I kept telling myself. Although I was still committed to seeing this through to the end, I had no idea where to start. So, I took it back to my roots, my foundation. I began calling on God, pleading with Him to wake me from this nightmare, fix what was broken, direct my path, and somehow get me to graduation. It was the only thing I knew to do. In my agonizing cry for help, a voice echoed in my direction, saying, "How may I help you?" I didn't look up right away because there was no way she was talking to me. With my head in my hands, I was slumped over, having a "Come to Jesus" meeting with the Lord Himself. Surely, she was addressing one of the many students pushing their way through the crowded lobby. But when I looked up, I caught a blurry view of the receptionist looking directly at me. I hadn't noticed her, or much of anything else, when I occupied the bench right beside her desk. Wiping my eyes to ensure that she was indeed talking to me, I sat straight up and responded, still holding back tears, "I don't know. I was here to talk to my advisor, but that didn't go well, and now I'm literally lost with no direction." Before I finished my emotional explanation, she replied, "Would you like to see someone else?" At the exact same moment, the office bell rang, and a distinguished-looking man walked out with a stack of files in his hands. As he placed the pile on the desk, the receptionist greeted him and asked, "Dr. Hall, can you please help this young lady?" He looked in my direction, gave a welcoming smile, and said, "Sure, follow me into my office." Though still not quite in my right frame of mind, I was coherent enough to know that I wouldn't get anywhere sitting in the hallway. So, as quickly as I fell into that seat, not even 10 minutes before, I jumped up like Paul, with fire shut up in my bones, and followed this unfamiliar man into his office.

As I walked through the door, Dr. Hall immediately asked, "What can I help you with?" Still reeling from that foolishness that I had recently experienced with the last advisor, I was in no mood to explain the situation, from start to finish, to this person I didn't know, who didn't know me, and who may not even be able to help me. So, very abruptly and probably with a little bit of attitude, I said, "I need to change my major." "Okay. Have a seat and tell me how I can help you?" he reiterated. Now, my facial expressions have never been good at playing hide and seek, so I'm sure it was apparent, at the moment, that I was fit to be tired. For the next 15 steps I took toward the oversized leather chair next to his desk, I weighed my options on how to respond. "I just told you. Were you not listening?" was the first thing that came to mind, but I was smart enough to know not to burn bridges I hadn't even crossed yet. I needed this man's help, so I had to calm the rage that was building up inside me before I said something I would regret later. I began repeating to myself, "Breathe, girl, breathe.

Graduation is the goal, and he could help you get there." I took a deep breath as I sat down and answered, "Well, Dr. Hall, the thing is, I'm not sure how you can help me. I've already spoken with an advisor, who was less than helpful. And no disrespect to you, sir, but aren't you just another advisor?" With a slight grin on his face, he replies, "I hate to disappoint you, but no, I'm not "just another advisor." Actually, I'm the Political Science Department Chair." I'm so glad I was already sitting down because that caught me totally off guard. OMG! Lil ole' me was sitting in the department chair's office and had his undivided attention. This was a game-changer, and I was here for it, especially after the day I'd been having. I was instantly filled with hope for the future.

Graduation, law school, and anything else I reached for...the view didn't look quite as foggy as it had about an hour ago. I almost couldn't contain my excitement...but I did. "Then, sir, it appears you can help me," I responded, fighting back what I thought maybe premature enthusiasm. "I need to enroll in your department's summer session, more specifically, in this particular major. However, I've been informed that I have missed the enrollment deadline." "Okay, for which classes?" he quickly asked, with pen in hand, ready for my response. But since I wasn't expecting to get this far into the process, I suddenly found myself speechless, which was rare. My brain had seemingly gone on strike without notice, so, in shock, I blurted out (in my "homegirl" voice), "Wow! Just like that?" Dr. Hall looked up from writing and chuckled (probably because of my less-than-proper reply), then said, "No, not really, Ms. Mackey. It's gonna take a little more than that. But how will I help you if I don't know what you need?" "Yes, sir. You are absolutely right," I acknowledged as I sat back in the seat, feeling slightly more relaxed than when I walked in. "Since I'm changing my major, I would think from the beginning...I guess." Noticing that I didn't have a clue as to what I needed, Dr. Hall turned toward his computer, began typing, and said, "Well, let's take a look." After a few clicks of his mouse, he turns to me and, in a stern voice, states, "The political science program is uniquely set up to help students successfully complete the curriculum. This is not to say that all other departments and degrees aren't invested in students' success; however, how we organize the classes is essential to the learning process. Unfortunately, most of the prerequisites are taught during the fall semester." I felt as if I had been slapped in the face AGAIN! I knew that my enthusiasm was premature.

How could it be possible to complete the full study for a

new major in less than a year? I inadvertently allowed my chin to fall slightly to my chest. Although I didn't say a word, the flood of anger and emotion was definitely written all over my face. Not fazed by my pouting, Dr. Hall turned back to his computer and asked, "You giving up?" Shocked by his nononsense response, I said, "No. It just seemed like I heard this already today. I was hoping to hear something different." He instantly stopped typing, peeped over his gold-framed reading glasses, and smiled. Then, in a less intimidating voice, he said, "If I may, I would like to make some suggestions to ensure you have a smoother process and transition this time around. Is this also something you've already heard, Ms. Mackey?" The lump in my throat made it hard to speak, but I responded slowly, saying, "No sir, I haven't, Dr. Hall. No, I haven't."

Other than the sound of Dr. Hall typing, the large room remained silent for what seemed like forever. When he finally turned his chair around, he handed me a sealed envelope and instructed me to take it to the registrar's office. "Time is of the essence here, Ms. Mackey," he says as he gets up from his desk. "So, when you get there, ask for Ms. Cody. She leaves at 5 pm...so you have an hour." I was still a little uncertain, but what did I have to lose at this point? So, I made my trek across campus to the registrar's office, as instructed.

When I arrived, it was packed. But of course, it was... why wouldn't it be? It was simply the kinda day I was having. As I pushed through the crowded corridor, I thought, "How can this be? It's the end of the semester. Why is this office packed like this? There's no way this many people are having issues at the end of the year. At this rate, I'll never get there in time. I'm screwed!" This was some bull, but I kept going. Annoyed that yet another person I didn't know held my fate in their hands, I took a chance and walked to the receptionist's desk, praying it wasn't too late. "Ms. Mackey to see Ms. Cody," I said confidently to the student aid standing behind the desk. "Have a seat," she instructed. Minutes later, I heard a soft voice say, "Ms. Mackey, Ms. Cody will see you now."

3

Favor AIN'T FAIR

R unning across campus and pushing my way through the crowded hallways had me looking a bit frazzled. So, as I followed behind the aid, I began straightening my clothes, patting my wind-blown hair back into place, and trying to smooth the wrinkles out of the envelope Dr. Hall had given me a few minutes earlier. On our way to God knows where, we passed the dreaded cubicles known to seal the fate of every student here on the sloping hills and verdant green of this campus. Most of us with HBCU experience understood that the registrar's office was where hopes and dreams came to either die or thrive. All I could think was, "Which one would determine my outcome today?" Surprisingly, we walked past them all, only stopping when we reached the office door at the end of the hall. The young student opened the door, ushered me in, and closed the door behind me.

I'd never been this far into the registrar's office building before, so I quickly scanned my surroundings, noticing first the desk plate that read *'Ms. Sandra Cody.'* Before taking another step, I was startled by a high-pitched voice saying, "Evening, Ms. Mackey. Do come in and have a seat. Sorry to keep you waiting. I hear you have a letter for me." The high-back office chair quickly spun around, revealing the woman behind the sweet southern voice that greeted me. Her smile brought about an instant calm. After a few deep breaths, I remembered the manners my momma taught me and replied, "Yes, ma'am. Yes, I do." I handed her the letter as I began to take my seat, thinking to myself, "What God has for me is for me!"

I sat quietly thinking, praying, and preparing for the worst when Ms. Cody broke her silence and said, "So I hear you need to change your major...in your Senior year. I won't ask if you're sure because it's obvious that this is not a choice." "No, ma'am, it's not," I responded, taking a deep breath. The noticeable concern in her voice indicated that she was aware of the severity of the situation and was more than ready to help. Suddenly, I felt calmer than I had all day.

"Well, today is your lucky day, my dear," Ms. Cody started after a brief pause. "While you were waiting, Dr. Hall briefed me on the circumstances and what you needed. He knew I was the only one here who could facilitate these types of moves within class registration. The letter he sent requested that I do whatever it takes to ensure you are enrolled in the summer session and all of your required fall classes. So, with that being said, let's get to it."

The next few minutes were intense as Ms. Cody worked on her computer and simultaneously sorted through the paperwork on her desk. What I thought would take all day took her less than twenty minutes. When she was finished, she spun her chair around again and folded her hands on the stack of papers in front of her. "Okay, Ms. Mackey," she began again, "you have now been enrolled in the suggested summer courses and all of your fall semester classes." I couldn't believe my ears. I moved to the edge of my seat to make sure I heard her correctly. "It's done?" I asked skeptically. "Yes, ma'am. All done," she answered as she put my papers in the same envelope I had given her earlier. Once again, I found myself speechless.

Unable to formulate a complete sentence and on the verge of tears, I could only say, "Thank you so much, Ms. Cody. I'm not sure what you did, but Thank You!" Ms. Cody walked around her desk and handed me the envelope. Before walking away, she said, "I want to encourage you, Ms. Mackey. Life will throw you curves. While in those curves, your response will determine your outcome. Stay inspired and let go of what could've or should've happened. Deal with it and move on. It's up to you now. Good luck." Little did I know that luck was not at all what I needed. Nothing could have prepared me for what was to come.

4

BEFORE THE *Storm*

◆

I had dodged a major bullet. Although the enemy tried to block me, I was determined not to be defeated. Due to this slight derailment, I was no longer on track to graduate in 2000; however, with God's favor (favor ain't fair!), I started working towards my new major in a new degree program over the summer in order to graduate in 2001.

With this issue now behind me, it was time to blow off some steam, and what better place than the beach...Myrtle Beach, to be exact! It was Memorial Day Weekend, 1999. I was enjoying the beach, trying to have some fun, and not thinking about my soon-to-be nonexistent social life that awaited me at school.

One day, as I was hanging out with my girls, walking the strip, and living what we thought was our "best life," he and his crew rode by on their bikes. Oh, how I loved motorcycles. I've had a fascination with them since I was a child. But my focus instantly shifted when we caught each other's eye, and he smiled. He was handsome. His complexion was the perfect shade of caramel, not too light but just slightly overheated. He had a bald head and pearly white teeth. And for the record, pearly whites get me every time! In my world, a pretty smile will always allow you to skip to the front of the line. I remember telling my girlfriends, "Y'all catch his teeth!" They laughed, as usual, at my method of selection while we watched him and his crew slowly coast past us. We definitely noticed.

For those unfamiliar, the slow stroll down the strip was customary. It was reminiscent of a buffet line, and the "roll by" was an opportunity to scope out the spread before making a choice. Once in a while, someone in the bike crew would break rank and pull over to "shoot their shot." But let's not get it twisted...the bikers weren't the only ones making moves. The women also made it their business to holla', wink, and wave. With thousands converging on the Myrtle Beach strip daily during Black Bike Week, it was no time to be shy. Everyone had to have a now-or-never attitude since there was no guarantee that they would ever see that person again.

As we continued walking the strip, doing our own surveillance, I heard one of my girls yell, "Hey ladies, we ridin'!" That was part of our code...No one ever rode off with anyone by themselves. If one was riding, we all were riding, so they'd better have a big enough crew. It was our way of guaranteeing each other's safety and making sure we all stayed together. So, we headed towards my friend, who was now engaged in conversation with the "rank breaker." The closer we got, the clearer it became to him that if he wanted a new companion to show off on the back of his bike, he would need his crew to come through and assist. Remember…no one rides alone. He immediately jumped on his cell phone and drove away in less time than it took him to dial. We assumed he was going to retrieve his "band of merry men" and would soon return. But instead of standing on the curb waiting for them to roll up, we began walking down the strip in search of a more appropriate pickup spot, like the hotel parking lot.

The bikes started to pull in, one for each of us. "Mr. Pretty Teeth," the one that I noticed earlier, pulled into the parking lot with the others and, like a respectful "host," smiled and said, "I hear you need a ride." I looked around to confirm he was with the other bikers, then responded (trying not to seem eager or pressed), "Only if you're offering out of want and not out of obligation. He flashed that smile again and said, "Cute," as he was already prepped and ready for me to get on. I took my place on the back like a pro…as if this was something I did all the time. He was clearly not impressed because he made sure to go over some "how-to-ride" pointers with me before we pulled off. Wondering if this was his standard protocol, I asked, "You do this for all the girls you ride?" "Not everyone," he replies, showing me those pearly whites once more before pulling the face shield down on his helmet. I was officially intrigued. This was panning out to be a great Bike Week.

5

DON'T LET THE *Smooth* TASTE FOOL YOU

◆

With the first summer school session behind me, I felt great about how things were going as I entered the second session. Clearly, that Memorial Day weekend was precisely the rejuvenation I needed. What made it even sweeter was the "out-of-the-blue" call I got from Mr. Pretty Teeth. I almost forgot we had exchanged numbers. We had only had a few conversations since Black Bike Weekend that didn't go beyond the regular, "How ya been? Whatcha been up to?" Even though we spent most of our time together in Myrtle Beach, I wasn't pressed to stay in touch because long-distance "situationships" were not my thing. But what the heck? Why not chat it up a bit, shoot the breeze, and have a few laughs? Harmless fun.

I answered the phone, pretending not to recognize the 201 area code. "Hello?" I said slowly. The deep voice quickly responded, "Wow! I guess you forgot about me." Trying not to give myself away, I pushed back my giggle, and in my "no-nonsense homegirl" voice, I replied, "Who is this?" I may have even rolled my neck and eyes when I said it. "Seriously?" he said, sounding both shocked and annoyed at the same time. After a few seconds of silence, I laughed and said, "Jackson, of course I know it's you." "Oh, okay. I was about to say..." he replied with hesitation. I assured him that I was only joking, and he claimed that he figured as much, but I swear I heard him suck those pretty teeth at me before I came clean.

Jackson and I engaged in about 30 minutes of small talk, as usual, and right before I hit him with, "Well, it was great hearing from you," he went off script. Before I realized it, he interrupted my signature goodbye and asked, "You have plans this weekend?" Without even thinking, I answered, "No." "Great! I want to see you and take you out on a proper date," he said quickly. I could hear the enthusiasm in his voice, which intrigued me. "Oh really?" I questioned. "Yes, really, " he confirmed. "I would come and pick you up, but since I don't have your address, how about meeting me at the restaurant or the lobby of my hotel?" Now, as a reminder, up to this point, I had merely been "chatting it up, shooting the breeze, having a few laughs." Then suddenly, it dawned on me that Jackson...Mr. Pretty Teeth...was asking me out for real. This was different than a "bike ride on the strip" date, and I was down for it. I agreed to meet him in the hotel lobby. After a bit more back-and-forth banter, we finalized the other details before ending the call. Then I stood still for a moment, looking at my phone with this silly little grin, thinking to myself...Hmmm, harmless fun, right?

He was already waiting in the lobby when I arrived at the hotel. I walked toward the lounge area where he was sitting, and when I was in earshot, I softly said, "You expecting someone?" "Ummm, maybe," he responded, looking up wide-eyed and smiling. I swear my knees buckled a bit from the sight of those glistening teeth. I tried to maintain my "unshakeable" façade, but it was too much to take in all at once. Before I knew it, I broke character and returned an equally impressive smile. However, I peeped Jackson's willingness to play along. I ain't gonna lie; I was impressed. He was quick on his feet and not stuffy, so our evening went off without a hitch. We talked a lot during dinner and then strolled down Franklin Street to finish our night. It was a nice change of pace from my less-than-glamorous, bookworm lifestyle. I gave our actual first date an A.

Jackson was persistent and charming, and I was drawn to him. Maybe it was his accommodating nature, how safe I felt with him, and the effort he put into showing me that he was serious about us. Whatever the allure, I was definitely digging it all. It seemed *sooo* right…which was, honestly, very unnerving.

We spent the next month visiting one another when our schedules allowed. During one of his visits, Jackson and I decided to be exclusive. This meant that we had reached a point in our relationship where we wanted to *really* focus on getting to know each other better and start building a firm foundation that would hopefully lead to us planning a future together. Gone were the days that I was going to be involved with a player or a liar. I had been hurt enough by people who presented themselves one way and ended up being the opposite. I had enough heartbreak…been there, done that, and had the scars to show for it. But this time, it was going to be different…He promised.

The Fall Semester was off to a good start. I was adjusting nicely to my new major. Everything was falling right in line regarding my academics. However, I had little time for anything outside of school and work. But, as soon as my schedule opened up, Jackson came to visit. I was more than ready to get out of the house, have some fun, and flaunt my new outfit. It had been a while since I had the opportunity to hang out, so I was eager to take full advantage of what the night had in store.

Once dressed, I did a final twirl in the mirror to ensure everything was on point. I must say I was impressed. I looked good! My roommate's boyfriend even slipped up and said, "DAMN!!" as we were headed out the door. He took the words right out of my mouth. I chuckled to myself because although my confidence level was already pretty high, that took it over the top. So, from the apartment door to the car, I was like Naomi Campbell on the catwalk of a fashion show...wings and all. You couldn't tell me anything. However, the innocent comment must have rubbed Jackson the wrong way because, as we headed to the car, he suggested I go back and change. My immediate thought was, "Chile, Bye!" I was in my zone and was unphased by the negativity. So, without breaking my stride, I laughingly replied, "Oh, that's definitely not going to happen. Take his response as a compliment...I did." I waited for Him to open my door, then slowly got in, ensuring everything stayed "in place," like any great supermodel would.

We were escorted to a reserved table when we arrived at the club. The mood was electric, and the DJ was amazing. The beats and rhythms filled the room like smoke in a cigar lounge. He played all the right songs in precisely the right sequence to create an undeniable vibe that screamed, "SEX!". It was rhythmic foreplay, and everyone was aroused. Make no mistake, if you came alone, you definitely weren't going home empty-handed. The DJ was definitely an expert at musically manipulating a room. The floor stayed packed, and after a couple of drinks, we were ready to join in the mix. Jackson was smooth and confident in how he moved to the music and pulled me into his rhythm. Despite being 10 years my senior (he was in his mid-30s, and I was in my early 20s), he definitely let me know he was in his element and in control. Our connection was intoxicating; together, we were pure FUN. After what seemed like 30 minutes of nonstop dancing, we retired to our table to catch our breaths. Jackson excused himself to go to the restroom while I indulged in a much-needed cocktail and continued watching the crowd sway to the beats like an ocean wave.

My rhythm was quickly interrupted by a luscious scent that entered my airspace long before its owner did. As I turned my head in pursuit of the aroma, I was greeted by a *SIMPLY BEAU-TI-FUL* man who took the liberty of sitting at my table. I don't know if I was more taken aback by his boldness or his handsome face. However, before I could make that determination, he introduced himself and expressed his admiration for my moves on the dance floor. He also added that, in his opinion, my current "suitor" was not to the standards that I deserved and assured me that he would be the better choice. Umm... bold, unapologetic, and, oh, did I mention GORGEOUS! I liked it! I instantly contemplated my earlier decision to be exclusive with Jackson. So much so that his absence from our table was no longer a thought. But as soon as my mind wandered, Jackson appeared from the smoky haze (like in one of those movies) and placed two drinks on the table. Like with everything about this brother, his timing was perfect. By the time Jackson put the glasses down and turned to "flex" on the unwanted visitor, dude had slid me his business card and excused himself. But despite his smooth exit, Jackson was having none of it. He hurried behind the man and tapped him on the shoulder. I rushed in to intervene, hoping to avoid a scene, grabbing Jackson by the hand. I lovingly but forcefully pulled him away and walked him back to the table to finish our drinks. As I sipped my blood-orange sangria, I felt my rhythmic energy returning, and I was not about to waste it refereeing a boxing match between grown men. Once Jackson calmed down, I ushered him back onto the floor to dance the rest of the night away.

As the evening progressed, the DJ continued to rev things up. He was hitting on all cylinders and showed no signs of stopping. For me and Jackson, we were back to our "happy place," in a good rhythm and seemingly with all things forgotten. At least that's what I thought until "Mr. Beautiful" and his dance partner stepped onto the floor. Suddenly, I was caught in the middle of a dance-off I hadn't agreed to participate in. Still, there's something to be said about testosterone and competition. The "interaction" definitely put Jackson in the "I can show you better than I can tell you" mode and created the perfect storm that I was more than happy to be caught up in. Our "late night until early morning" actions were Jackson's way of showing me why he *was* up to my standards. As we snuggled together, I smiled and thought, "Thanks, Mr. Beautiful, for setting this fire!" And boy, what a fire it was. I definitely gave him an A that night!

It was almost noon when I sat up from what seemed similar to a coma-like sleep, only to see that my "dance partner" was still knocked out. But that was fine with me because the only plan I had on my agenda for the day was to recover from last night. However, as I attempted to curl back under the covers, trying my best not to wake Jackson, the doorbell chimed. I gently leaned over and peeped out the window, checking for my roommate's car. I knew that if she was home, whoever was at the door would be there to see her. Unfortunately, she wasn't there, so I had to get up. That definitely wasn't in my plans for the day. I sighed and groaned as I slid from the bed, put on my robe, and dragged myself down the hallway to answer the door. "This better be an emergency," I thought as I shuffled my feet on the tiled floor. When I FINALLY got there (it was probably less than 30 seconds), I stood on my tippy toes to see out the peephole. I had a burst of energy when I realized it was Vincent, my brother from another mother, standing on the other side. With all that was going on, I had forgotten that he was coming over to drop off a pair of jeans he custom-made for me to wear at his upcoming fashion show. I was so excited to see him. I invited him in and told him to make himself at home while I got dressed. We were about to cut up!

When I returned to my bedroom, Jackson had awakened from his deep sleep and was sitting in bed. Without even a "Good Morning" or "Hey Baby," he suddenly started accusing me of having another dude on the side. I was completely caught off guard and immediately angered by his statement. If he had any doubt about how I felt at that very moment, my glaring facial expression erased it all. I kept getting dressed, thinking to myself, "How dare this fool question me in my own house?! Exclusive or not, he don't know me like that!" I tried to keep my thoughts from escaping through my lips but was unsuccessful. I pushed my feet into my slippers, and as I made my way back to the living room, I calmly replied, "That would be mighty bold of me, now wouldn't it?" without looking back or waiting for a response. Vincent clearly heard the brief conversation, picking up on Jackson's hostile tone, and immediately began apologizing for interrupting. I waved off his apology and continued with our "sibling" visit. We did what Vincent and I do...laughed and joked about everything under the sun. It was always a fun time.

Jackson made his entrance as I was walking Vincent to the door. In proper Southern fashion, Vincent introduced himself, only to be left ignored. He took that as his cue to leave. He apologized again and said a quick goodbye as he walked backward out the door, giving me his "Big Brother Look of Concern." I gave him my "It's all good" wink and closed the door because it was about to go down... and not in a good way.

I couldn't get to Jackson fast enough. "That was really rude," I blurted out. "How dare you act like that! Who do you think you are, man?" By this time, we were eye to eye, and that "late night until early morning" energy had turned into "pissed off female" energy, and he was fitna' get all of it! I waited for his explanation or his apology, but all I got was, "Imma ask you again...Who was that?" I guess he felt intimidated...again and needed to show me who was in charge...again. But he clearly had no idea who he was messing with. I pinched my lips together, gave a slight nod, added my signature "half-a-grin," then condescendingly replied, "Sooo, the dead air that filled the room when he introduced himself kept you from catching his name? Umm." I made sure he could see me roll my eyes as I turned to walk into my room because I was done talking about this. Jackson followed behind me, on my heels the whole way. "So, you're not going to tell me who he is?" he persisted. I stopped in my tracks and took a deep breath before turning to respond. "Jackson, are you accusing me of something?" I asked. "Why won't you tell me?" he interrupted. "Okay, Jackson," I said as I took another deep breath to gain my composure. "His name is Vincent, and there's nothing else to tell you. Now, you can accept that, or you can grab your things and get started on that eight-hour drive back home before traffic really gets bad. Either way, I'm done talking about this non-issue." And as quick as the argument started, it was over. He went from insecure boyfriend to Myrtle Beach's "Mr. Pretty Teeth" in 10 seconds flat. He grabbed my hand as I went to walk away and quickly stuttered, "I'm... I'm sorry. I don't know why I'm tripping. Will you forgive me?" I gave him a long eye roll, letting him know I was far from okay with what happened.

But since he seemed to have come to his senses fairly quickly, I tried to put this foolishness behind us. "Ahhh...Sure, Jackson. Whatever." I huffed, fighting back the urge to jerk my hand away. He had better be glad he was so sexy and had provided a stellar performance a couple of hours earlier. If I wasn't as satisfied with what he was giving, his dismissal would have been immediate...'cuz I was not the one!

6

A TRICK *Or* A TREAT

A fter Jackson left, I sat around chillin' in my apartment, humming the music from last night's dynamic playlist. The ring of my phone startled me and interrupted my "Deborah Cox moment." "Hey, sis, can you talk?" the voice asked softly, almost whispering. Kinda confused about the line of questioning, I responded, "Yes. Why you ask that?" "Guurrll," Vincent replies in his regular tone, "by the way your man was acting, I wasn't sure if you were good or not. So, I'm calling to check on you and apologize again if I caused any issues." "No need to apologize. It's all good," I assured him. "You sure? He seems really jealous," Vincent said in a more serious tone. "Be careful with him. I don't want to cause another break-up." "Vincent, what are you talking about? Who you out there 'breaking up'?" I asked, trying to hold in the laughter. "You ain't know?" he giggled. "Them boys stay putting dirt on my name. One minute, I'm gay, and the next, I'm taking your girl…not on purpose, though! I didn't know I was so popular!" Neither of us could hold back the laughter any longer and had a good hard chuckle about it all. We talked for another hour without even realizing it. As Vincent and I finally said our goodbyes, he quickly went from clowning to serious, saying, "Sis, please be careful with him. He's giving dangerous jealousy vibes." I was slightly taken aback by the worry in his voice, but I knew his comments were coming from a place of love. "Of course I will," I responded, assuring Vincent his concerns were duly noted. When I hung up and glanced at the clock, I realized I hadn't heard from Jackson. It was odd that he hadn't called yet, but not so out of the ordinary that I was overly bothered.

While I was preparing for bed, my phone rang. Without a "Hello," "Hey Babe," or anything, Jackson blurts out, "So you weren't going to call and check on me?" Ignoring his attempt to argue, I calmly asked, "Have you made it back home safely?" "Yes," he said sharply. "Good," I replied while yawning. "Now I'm about to go to bed, so I'll talk to you tomorrow. Have a good night, Jackson." Sounding annoyed, he quickly chimed in, "No 'I love you'?" I let out a big "HA!" thinking, "He can't be serious!" But when I realized he was, I responded, "Naw Boo, we ain't there yet. Goodnight." I didn't even wait for a response before hanging up.

Over the next month, I became so busy with school and work that my time with Jackson seemed like a fun fling...something that just happened...which I was okay with. However, I often found myself thinking about the great times Jackson and I had together, leaving me with a big smile on my face. Yet, with everything else going on around me, I made sure not to get too caught up in those moments. I adopted the mindset, "It was what it was, and Imma keep it pushing." However, Jackson apparently didn't share the same sentiments because, to my surprise, he took the liberty of flying me out to see him during Labor Day weekend. And although my schedule was tight, I was ready for a break, so off I went.

This North Carolina-born and raised country girl, who had never been anywhere North of Virginia, was, at the tender age of 21, in the big city for the first time. I was in Jersey City, NJ, like a fish out of water. And instantly, the smell let me know that "we weren't in Kansas anymore!" It reeked! But despite the stench, Jackson was the perfect host and tour guide. He proudly showed me around Jersey and New York, "his cities," as he always called them. Since it was my first time in Manhattan, I was utterly intoxicated by all the vibes it gave.

Everything about these cities was aggressively alluring, and Jackson took full advantage of its noticeable effects on me. He was different; he seemed more confident than before, proving he was definitely in his element. I was like a kid at

Christmas. My "Big City" wish list was long, and thanks to Jackson, I checked off boxes, one by one. I rode the subway, ate at the best local spots, took in the sights, went on a picnic, and rode under the Jersey City stars on Jackson's motorcycle. And who knew the city had such beautiful parks...not this country girl. I had the best time. Jackson's main focus was ensuring that my first Jersey City weekend with him was memorable, and he succeeded. He pulled out all the stops just for me. I was stimulated in every way, mentally, physically, and especially sensually. I was a bit shocked that this man, who, again, was 10 years my senior, was accomplishing what few others have ever come close to. Although dating older guys was not new to me, this one was different. It was like he had a blueprint of my mind, and I succumbed to his every move. As I sat in my window seat on my return flight, I knew, without a doubt, that this impromptu trip was exactly what I needed, everything I hoped for and one I would never forget. He sent me back home "done in" and very satisfied. This lingering feeling of exhilaration would get me over the hump until my Thanksgiving holiday/Fall Break.

7

LOOK WHO'S COMING TO *Dinner*

Acouple of my homegirls from back home decided we should check out this new club. I was so looking forward to a night out on the town with them. Since I wasn't familiar with the club scene here anymore, I left the details to the crew, and they didn't disappoint. They chose a nice up-and-coming spot downtown. The city was finally accommodating the young adult crowd, and everyone was taking notice.

The club scene was jumpin', and the place was packed. It was absolutely what I needed to take my mind off the previous foolishness! I saw old friends and even old flames...you know, those exes that always seem to forget why they are exes and want to try to rekindle what once was… in the middle of a club's dance floor. Yeah… those "old flames." One brave soul tried to shoot his played-out shot, but luckily, my girls whisked me away before he really started feeling himself. To tell the truth, it was for the best because he couldn't handle me back then, and he sho'nuff wasn't ready for the **ME** standing in front of him now. So, I politely gave him the "Hi & Bye" wave as I did the Spike Lee float across the dance floor to the other side of the club. It was, without a doubt, a night to remember. We had a ball!

After leaving the club, the crew and I went to Jimmy the Greek, a local 24-hour diner back home, to get something to eat. With all of our shenanigans, we had worked up quite an appetite. Right as we were seated, I heard my phone ring. Usually, a 2 AM phone call is self-explanatory; however, in this case, a booty call was automatically ruled out since Jackson wasn't local or within a 30-minute drive, which is, of course, the OFFICIAL BOOTY CALL RULES (in case you didn't know). I was curious as to who in the world would be calling me now, so I answered it. "Hello, sexy," replied the sultry voice on the other end. "Hello," I responded in my extra sexy voice. I knew right away that Jackson was trying to disguise his voice, but he was failing badly. Some things are hard to hide, and for him, his northern accent gave him away. Seeing that he was really into it, I wouldn't state the obvious, so I played along and let him continue. "What are you doing?" he asked, still "in character." I, too, turned on the charm as a convincing player in his "game." "I'm out with my girls, about to eat," I answered inquisitively, further encouraging his playfulness. "I want to see you," Jackson announced, not letting go of his new persona. "OK," I conceded with a bit of hesitance,

not sure where this was going. He said again, "I want to see you."
He had certainly sparked my interest, making me too anxious to
keep up the charades. I needed to know what he was up to.
"Jackson!" I declared, letting him know that the jig was up,
"Where are you?" "Close," he responded, still in character. "Close
where? Here?" I asked, officially confused and looking around the
restaurant. At this point, I was skeptical. Was he playing another
mind game or seriously lurking somewhere, watching
me? Jackson stated again, "I wanna see you," still not answering
my question. "OK, where?" I finally asked. Those must have been
the words he was waiting to hear because he began to rattle off an
address to a hotel off the main strip, not far from my mom's
house. OMG! He was in Winston!

Coming to my hometown without telling me was
definitely a statement move on his part, but what statement was
he trying to make? I never suggested he visit me during my break,
nor had we reached that level in our "dealings" where relationship
negotiations had begun. So, what was his play? Yeah, we'd have
fun when we were together, but I didn't think it would lead to
much more because of our age difference and the distance we
lived apart. This is why only my girlfriends knew of him. I hadn't
even told my family about him...about us. Purposely, Jackson
only knew basic information about me: where I was from, how

many siblings I had, and my current educational status. All I knew of him was that he was born and raised in Jersey City, NJ; he was the only child, his parents were still living, he was a logistic engineer, and he had no kids (NO BABY MOMMA DRAMA!). So, what was this all about? Part of me wanted to get to the bottom of this mystery, but the other part...the 99% part...just wanted to have fun on my birthday. Everything else could wait 'til tomorrow. I hung up the phone and told my girls what was up. I gave them the necessary information (girl code requirement) in case something went wrong. When we finished our breakfast, they dropped me off at the hotel.

8

Officially OFFICIAL

◆

I got out of the car at the hotel, scanning the area around me, still unsure what Jackson was up to or if I should have even agreed to meet him. But I was here now, so it was his time to really win me over. Those pretty teeth were only going to get him but so far. I knocked on the room door, and to my surprise, he quickly opened it as if he were watching for me through the peephole. He stepped to the side and ushered me into the candlelit room. "Well, Happy Birthday To Me!" I said to myself. WOW! Jackson definitely put in some work to show me that he was genuinely interested in being more than just my "guy"; he was ready to be my "man."

Since day one, Jackson never shied away from expressing his feelings and his desire to be "The One." That night, there was no question that he felt we had moved past the exclusivity phase; he did everything to remove any doubt that he *was* my future. Although I was a little put off by his unexpected visit, it wasn't enough of an issue for me not to be enticed by his confidence and charm. So, of course, I gave in.

We were now officially official, planning our next steps together. If I'm being honest, it wasn't only the romance of the evening that put him over the top. During our "exclusive time," he was consistent and straightforward, with a no-nonsense approach to our relationship; the exact opposite of the guys I dated before. His passion for things outside our dealings was equally intense, captivating, and unmatched. I was sold. We celebrated our status change with "Breakfast in Bed," which took on a whole new meaning for me. I made sure to "compliment" the chef.

Initially, I was anxious about taking our relationship a step further. However, in one night, Jackson showed me a different side of himself. Now, having a new perspective, I couldn't wait to usher him into the next phase of "Dating Me 101,"…meeting the Queen, herself…my mom. So, off to the "Queendom" we went!

This was a HUGE move for me. Mom had met the guys I dated in high school and was only very fond of one. But when he broke my heart, he broke hers, too. From that moment on, she didn't get invested; she just took her cues from me. Although I was so excited for Jackson to meet her and the rest of the family, I knew she wouldn't let her guard down too quickly. Mom wouldn't show her hand until she knew it was worth it.

From the start, Jackson laid on the charm with my mom, stepfather, and baby sister. Mom seemed impressed, and my sister was glued to his hip. My stepfather even fell into his trap. They laughed and talked about any and everything. Jackson's magnetic personality seemingly won them all over, boosting his confidence even more. He seemed unusually proud of his "performance," which was somewhat unnerving. However, I didn't dwell on it. I filed it away in my "mental rolodex" as another thing about him that I wasn't going to waste time figuring out. I chalked it up as Jackson being Jackson.

His last evening in Winston was spent having dinner with my family. He left to go back to Jersey City early the next morning. His departure marked the end of my Thanksgiving break, so I returned to my apartment to resume my regularly scheduled programming...classes were back in session! Jackson and I talked every day and night without fail. Things were going so well; I wouldn't have changed a thing.

9

THE *Turning* OF THE TIDES

◆

B efore I knew it, winter break arrived in overdrive, but I was determined to make the most of it. I spent my off time between North Carolina and New Jersey, enjoying my family and my man. When New Year's rolled around, I spent it in the big city of Jersey City. It was awesome! Jackson knew it would be difficult to get over to Manhattan, and he didn't want the chaos to detract from my experience. So, we said goodbye to 1999 and brought in 2000 on a firework dinner cruise down the Hudson River. This man was spoiling me, and I was loving every minute of it.

This break was definitely what I needed. To ensure I graduated next year, I had been carrying a full class load through the Fall and Spring semesters. Much of my time and concentration focused on making sure I remained an above-average student, which was nothing new. As a student-athlete during high school, I became well-versed in focusing intensely on very little sleep. So, I was more than prepared for the grind of college.

I felt like a pro juggling work, school, and Jackson (according to him). I must say, he could be pretty needy at times. Although he knew my schedule and how important graduation was to me, he still assumed someone else was occupying my time. The long-distance aspect of our relationship didn't make things easier. Maybe he was displaying his "only child---focus on me" tendencies, or it could have been his insecurities getting the best of him. Whatever it was, it was not attractive, and I wasn't feeling it!

Jackson was moving fast, very fast. *His* plans for us were at the forefront of *his* mind, while graduating was at the forefront of mine. The sad part is that he knew from the very beginning what my plans were, but he never really filled me in on his. He would often talk about marriage and kids, which, for me, was not in my foreseeable future. Yes, I had every intention of becoming a wife and a mother, but not right now. Several times, I had to remind him that my aspirations stretch farther than an undergraduate degree. I was working so hard nowadays to keep my grades up because law school was next on my list.

MY plans for MY future were the source of many (if not all) of our arguments. Jackson was established in his career and felt like we were ready to get married and start a family. I disagreed. Our long-distance relationship gave him a false impression of how things would be once we were together full-time. Yes, it's true; absence makes the heart grow fonder, so you cherish the times together. However, it's also true that familiarity breeds contempt. We haven't even spent a significant amount of time under the same roof to be certain that we could co-exist. He wasn't thinking rationally. He wanted things his way, and he wanted it now. I wasn't trying to hear it, though. I was hell-bent on not putting myself on the back burner for no one and nothing. Being a wife and mother weren't my right-now aspirations; going to law school was. I often asked him if I was holding him up because I didn't want him to wait for me to make *his* dreams come true. He would always say no, but I didn't believe him. We eventually agreed that I would move to Jersey with him once I graduated. It was the only compromise that seemed to satisfy him...for the moment.

May 2000 was finally here, and although I knew ahead of time that I was not graduating, it still stung. I was, however, excited to have a true summer...one without attending classes, writing papers, or studying for exams. Thankfully, finals were a breeze, and I found myself with something I hadn't had in quite a while... I HAD TIME! And with that time, I chose to sit on "the yard" (outdoor chill area on campus) and take it all in. My first observation was that the yard was different than I remember. I saw some classmates that started here with me hustling around, preparing for graduation, while others were moving out of the dorms. And then there were those, like me, who had simply taken a space in the grass to relax and reflect on this last year.

I couldn't help but smile as I walked to my car, thinking, "I made it!" Despite the times when I felt I would succumb to the pressure and the stress of possibly failing or wanting to quit before I failed, I stayed strong, and now, here I am. The more I thought about it, the more emotional I became. The tears were uncontrollable. I was truly grateful for the journey. Up until this point in my life, staying diligent in my studies in the face of heartbreaking setbacks and distractions was the hardest thing I had to do. The injury I endured freshman year was a simple leg cramp in comparison. Yes, it ended my track career, but I rebounded and readjusted like a champ. This was different. This was personal. I was determined to break generational curses. I had already managed to avoid teenage pregnancy, and now I was on the verge of being the first of my parents' kids to graduate from college! I had a little sister, nieces, and nephews who would be looking up to me, and I wanted to tell a different story. I instantly felt assured that the work I had put in would manifest. It's like the old church song, *Let The Work I've Done, Speak For Me.*

10

HOME IS WHERE THE *Heart* IS

S ummer was here, and Jackson was talking more and more about marriage. Since he had been privileged to grace the presence of "The Queen," I decided it was time for him to meet my dad (my first love) and the other side of my family. I never brought a guy to meet my father, so this encounter was HUGE. For me, it meant more than he or Jackson could ever imagine. Yes, I've had boyfriends in the past and even found myself engaged to one of them. However, NONE of my previous "suitors" had the honor of standing face-to-face with "The Man" himself. I was a Daddy's girl, and although our relationship took a deep nosedive at one point (another traumatic story for another book), I still measured every man against him.

Jackson had only been privy to a select amount of information about me. I was somewhat guarded due to the overwhelming need to protect myself from the stupidity of others...a destructive human factor I was way too familiar with. Frankly, that shit almost broke my spirit. I thought I would never recover. The intense hurt I experienced damaged my life's intuitive sensors. I could only pray that someday I would be able to trust again. Therefore, I operated with everything being on a need-to-know basis. However, because I cared for Jackson and was excited about the path of discovery we had embarked on, I was willing to *gradually* open myself, my life, and my family up to him (though still very cautious).

He did well enough to leave the "queendom" (mom's house) with his head; now it was time to see how things would go when I introduced him to my dad. So, we took a trip to my childhood city; the birthplace of Cheerwine soda, where my mom and dad were born and raised and where my grandmothers raised, fed, and clothed me until I was seven.

Truth be told, I felt like I was walking Jackson into the "lion's den." I hoped everything would go well but was prepared for the worst. Even though Jackson and I had been together for over a year, if my dad disapproved, this relationship was a wrap...because his opinion mattered greatly to me.

My Dad loves family, and what he loves even more is getting together with them, other than at funerals. He preferred gatherings full of laughter rather than tears. He was famous for picking a day outta the blue to throw huge fish fry parties for everyone to come, eat, drink, and be merry. Everyone who has ever been to one will surely tell you that his fish fries were the best…A1 for sure! It just so happened that Jackson was in town during one of my dad's spontaneous throw-together gatherings, and I thought it would be a great time for them to meet. We drove down to Salisbury, NC, from Winston-Salem, NC. The 30–45-minute drive was full of stories about my childhood, requiring me to take him the scenic route so he'd get a little more insight into the essence of "Me." I was excited to show him my childhood home and share the memories we made there. I drove him through Heiligtown off Long St., the birthplace of both my parents. More importantly, this was where my grandma lived, in the home her father built, and where she raised her kids, me, my oldest sister, and much later, my cousins.

Driving down the narrow road, pointing out important landmarks, and telling Jackson the stories, I recalled my mother telling me where their old home was located. However, it could no longer be seen from the overgrown grass, trees, or woods. I couldn't contain my excitement as we turned onto the dirt road leading to my grandma's house. I could barely finish telling Jackson all about my childhood because of the giant smile on my face. But Jackson was clearly not feeling my enthusiasm. He actually looked puzzled by my giddiness. Didn't matter though…I was so happy…nothing was going to rain on my parade.

As we pulled up to my grandma's house, everything I saw brought back so many memories that I couldn't help but laugh. The white house with green shutters was always a comforting site to see. I pulled up into one of the two makeshift parking spaces created by the massive tree split; the one beside the ventless, brick BBQ grill they no longer used. My excitement went through the roof when I saw the other half-paved space occupied by my grandma's grey Buick Century. She was home!

Although we talked daily, it had been about six months or so since I had seen my grandma. "Jackson," I shouted with a child-like thrill, "Welcome to the house I grew up in!" Anxiously, I jumped out of the car and rushed to the door, looking back at Jackson, who clearly wasn't matching my stride. Before he even got to the porch, I was knocking on the screen door, opening it, and yelling, "Grandma!" all at the same time. As I walked through the front room and crossed the living room doorway, she sang out from her blue recliner as only MY grandma could, "Hel-l-o-o!". I ran over and hugged her real tight, but her embrace seemed to overpower mine, letting me know she was just as excited to see me as I was to see her.

"Well, who do we have here?" She said with a smile while looking at Jackson from head to toe. "Oh, Grandma, this is my boyfriend, Jackson," I proudly responded. "Well, Hello, Jackson.

Aren't you a handsome young man!" she replied, smiling at him even bigger than before. He returned her greeting with a soft "Hello" as if he was shy. Clearly, my grandma had caught him off guard. He soon realized that she was "old-school" and had no problem speaking her mind...a trait that was definitely passed down to me. Grandma invited Jackson to sit awhile and offered him something to eat and drink; it's the Southern way. After gazing at Jackson for a few seconds longer, she turned her attention to me, saying, "I didn't think you were going to make it down, but I'm glad you did." "Yes, ma'am. Me too! Daddy called and said he was having a family get-together and wanted to see me, so I cleared my schedule to get here," I explained excitedly. It was a win-win for me to be able to see my family and introduce Jackson at the same time. (Fingers crossed)

Not skipping a beat, Grandma turned her attention to Jackson. "So where you from, young man?" she asked. " Jersey City, New Jersey," he responded. "Ummm, OK," she mumbled before continuing her questioning. "So, you and my grandbaby go to the same school?" she asked, still digging for information. "No, Ma'am," Jackson responded. "Grandma, we met at the beach," I interjected, hoping to offer more details to her pressing questions. Cutting her eyes at me, she quickly responded, "I'm talking to Jackson." "Yes, Ma'am. OK," I respectfully replied, smiling and laughing to myself. I knew that was her way of saying "shut up" without saying it. In the hour or so that we visited with her, she jumped between several different subjects, squeezing out all the "necessary" information she needed and wanted to know without making Jackson feel as if he was being interrogated. When we were preparing to leave, I asked my grandma if she wanted to ride with us to my dad's house. She declined and said she would come later. I kissed her goodbye, and she slowly got up to walk us to the door. She looked at Jackson with her signature smile and said, "Hope to see you again." We both returned the smile (even though she wasn't talking to me) and headed to the car.

We pulled out of Grandma's driveway and were on to the next adventure...my dad's house. While driving down Long Street, I could still see the wooded path we always took to the corner store during my childhood. All of a sudden, the memories came rushing back. "Those were the days," I thought as we drove by. Then we slowly cruised through the old neighborhood and saw the house where my siblings and I, my Dad, my stepmom, and my second-grandma, Granny. (my stepmom's mother) used to live. Growing up, we called it "The Big Yellow House." It had a wraparound porch and a big backyard, and it's where a ton of great memories were made. At second glance, my childhood home wasn't quite as massive as it used to seem. It's funny how our view of life changes as we get older.

Finally, we arrived at my dad's. I was excited to show Jackson his garden, the chickens, and the pool/guest house my oldest brother used as his barbershop. While I was giving Jackson the tour, my dad came outside to meet us. This was the moment of truth...I was getting ready to introduce Jackson to the "The Man, The Myth, The Legend." I wasn't sure how it would go, but I was excited for the two to finally meet. And like the charmer Jackson was, he didn't disappoint. As soon as I made the introduction, Jackson stretched out his hand to my dad and gave him a stern handshake, saying, "It's a pleasure to meet you, Sir." Returning the stern handshake, my Dad replied, "Nice to meet you too...Jackson?" questioning if he was saying his name correctly. We got there before the crowd arrived, so there was plenty of time for my dad to do his "dad" thing and size Jackson up to make sure he was a suitable mate for his daughter.

My Dad invited Jackson outside while he prepared the grill and the fish fryer. I stayed in the house to give them time to talk and get to know each other better. Soon, the door opened, and Granny and my stepmom walked in. My stepmom yelled as loud as she could, "VICTORIA!" And in the same breath, while putting away her groceries, she said, "Oooo, Jackson is a handsome

61

young man. How long y'all been dating?" She stopped long enough so I could hug her and Granny, then I laughed and responded, "We've been together for a year." I started helping put the groceries away when my nieces and nephews ran into the house. I knew right then my sister and brothers were there...the commotion from the kids gave them away. Apparently, they had been outside chatting it up with Jackson for a while. Before too long, other family and friends made their way over, and the yard was full of people talking, laughing, and cracking jokes. It was great being around my family again.

The evening had ended, and most of the family was gone except my siblings, their kids, Jackson, and myself. We eventually navigated into the house with Dad, my stepmom, and Granny. We continued our casual conversations with the TV playing in the background and children running around. Occasionally, the focus turned to Jackson, which eventually led to a friendly Q&A. Although their questions were lighthearted, they were clearly trying to get a "read" on this guy who must have been special enough that I brought him home to meet the family (for the first time EVER!!!). My dad and brothers asked a lot about New Jersey, where he's from. And then they moved on to sports, talking about everything from baseball to basketball to football. When she could get a word in edgewise, my stepmom would chime in to ask

Jackson all kinds of things, like his hobbies and how we met. Jackson didn't seem to mind all the attention and got the rare opportunity to see me in my element.

Overall, the visit went as well as expected. My only regret was that I didn't have the opportunity to sit and talk with my dad like I wanted. I was anxious to know his thoughts about Jackson; a head nod, a wink, something that would ease my mind or stop me cold. This was a first for us…I've never brought anyone to meet him, and he's never met anyone I've dated. So now, at this point in my life, in this relationship, his opinion was a big deal. Unfortunately, I pulled out of his driveway with nothing. Maybe next time, Daddy.

11

Fallin' OUT

My summer break was about over, and boy, it was a whirlwind of fun! While visiting Jackson in Jersey, I got to meet his parents. His mom was as anxious as he was for him to settle down, get married, and "give her some grandbabies," as she put it. They were older than my parents (who were in their 40s), so I guess, in her eyes, the clock was ticking. However, the last thing on my mind was a clock, marriage, or giving anybody "some grandbabies." I was completely focused and ready to get this fall semester started. To me, this was my Deja Vu moment, and this time around, the ending of this saga would be different...better than before...finally a dream fulfilled. Jackson knew how important this semester was for me, so he didn't add any extra stress to my already stressful schedule. Thankfully, I refused to entertain any distractions, as I could see the finish line in the distance. I kept in constant communication with my advisor because there was no way I was going to let anything slip through the cracks or be overlooked this go 'round. As I said, I've been here before, so I had to do my part to guarantee a different outcome.

I was giving it my all, going hard in the books and taking no time to come up for air. When Fall break finally rolled around, I was so ready for the much-needed break. I planned to visit Jackson, but I also wanted to see Vincent since we hadn't talked since his summer internship turned into a dream job at a fashion institute back home in New York. Vincent always told everyone that he would be a famous clothing designer. He was clearly well on his way. So, of course, I had to make time to catch up with him.

"Vincent!" I sang out when he answered the phone. "What's up, sis!" He mimicked with the same enthusiasm. There was a brief conversation filled with a lot of laughing and giggling. I told him my plan to visit Jackson but wanted to see him beforehand. "Umm," he responded, "You sure Jackson is going to be OK with you visiting me?" "HA! What Jackson don't know won't hurt him," I quickly responded. We busted out laughing at the same time. Vincent knew me better than anyone and understood that if I said it, I meant it, so NOTHING or NO ONE was going to deter me from doing what I set my mind to do. "Okay, Gurl!" Vincent replied, still laughing, "If you say so! Just let me know when and where, and I'm there!" "You better know it!" I said with confidence, followed by more giggles. From there, it was set: a long-awaited date with my bestie. It had been a long time.

The drive up was smooth. I got to SoHo early enough to spend the entire day with Vincent. It was nice catching up and seeing how hard he had been grinding to make his fashion dreams come true. Our times together were always so genuine…uncensored conversations with unfiltered honesty, uncontrolled laughter (and sometimes tears), and pure, unadulterated fun! This time was no different, and I enjoyed every minute. My visit was even better because I wasn't rushing to get to Jersey since I never told Jackson when I was leaving. I figured I'd use one of his moves and pop up on him. So, I milked every moment with Vincent, and then we said our goodbyes. Vincent knew that my next destination was to see Jackson, so as I got in my car, I gave him Jackson's address and phone number and said, "Here's his location and contact info in case I don't make it back to Carolina…start the search there. I laughed as I buckled my seat belt, but when I looked up to say my final goodbye, Vincent wasn't laughing. "Umm, so not funny, Victoria! Sooo not funny," he yelled as I drove past. I guess my joke didn't go over too well.

To put it nicely, my drive to Jersey was an "interesting" one. If you ask me, people who live up north cannot, I repeat, cannot drive! I was almost in five accidents before I could even drive five blocks. As I pulled up to Jackson's condo building, I called Vincent to tell him I had made it safely, then called Jackson.

After a few rings, he answered, "Hey." "Hey there! You wanna come get my bag?" I replied in my bubbly voice. "Your bags?" He responded, sounding confused. "Yes. I'm outside," I said as I turned off the ignition. "Really? I wasn't expecting you until much later this evening." Jackson said slowly. "Yeah, my plans changed," I answered with a bit of an attitude. "Was I interrupting something?" "Of course not; why would you say that?" He asked. "Weeelll, you seemed more concerned with my ETA than the fact that I'm outside NOW," I answered with a little more attitude than before. I started gathering my things to get out of the car and noticed Jackson standing outside, surveying the area to see if I was really there. I think it's safe to say that my early arrival caught him off guard. I loves me a good "pop-up"!

Jackson had planned a weekend of complete pampering, and I was here for it. We literally didn't leave the condo. Our meals were delivered to the door every night, and he even scheduled a couple's massage, which was heaven. It was just what the doctor ordered, considering I'd spent the last couple of months of book-busting and paper-writing. I savored every peaceful minute of doing nothing, even if it was only for a short while.

As soon as I got home, I called Vincent to let him know I had returned safely. He was jokingly thrilled; at the time, I couldn't determine if his enthusiasm was genuine...but looking back at it,

I know it was. Jackson, however, was less than excited that I was back in Carolina. I didn't spend my entire break with him because I needed to get a head start on one of my many papers that were coming due. He wasn't as understanding as I hoped and didn't hide his emotions about it. I think the distance was finally getting to him, and his recent unattractive mood was a tell-tale sign. Who picks a fight with their significant other after such a lovely weekend? Jackson Reed, that's who! He would go from Sherman Klump -- kind-hearted, loving, and friendly -- to Buddy Love -- overly assertive and harsh. His dramatic mood swings often fueled our arguments. At one point, I went as far as to ask him if he was on steroids because, most of the time, he would lose his stuff over the littlest of things. His pettiness was unreal!

One of the things that attracted me to Jackson was his good looks. At 5'8, with dark brown skin, a bald head, a goatee, and an awe-inspiring body, I was a fan…a big fan. At the time, I thought, "Who in their right mind would not be taken aback by a beautiful face (with pretty teeth) and an incredible physique, sprinkled with unbelievable stamina?" And my answer was, "NOBODY!" (in my Keith Sweat voice). Unfortunately, he was obsessed with his looks as well.

Early on, Jackson shared with me that when he was younger, he was a big boy and got picked on and bullied. As a result, he started boxing and lifting weights, reducing his size considerably. This change opened the doors to new opportunities for Jackson. He began modeling and was an extra in a few films; something he was proud of. When I visited with his parents, we flipped through photo albums full of pictures of him from infancy to college. It was a great trip down memory lane. However, as much as it may have hurt to accept it, the truth was that the young, youthful teenage boy was no more. Jackson had completely erased any sign of him. Although he worked out every day (and it showed), it didn't seem enough for him or his aging body. Could this have been the reason for his unpredictable "crazy" episodes? Maybe. All I know is that this side of Jackson had me on high alert, and I was not too happy with it. His recent episodes made me ask myself, "Who in their right mind signs up to deal with crazy? And again, my answer was, *"NOBODY!"* (in my Keith Sweat voice).

12

IT'S A *Celebration*

I DID IT Y'ALL! It's Graduation Day, May 2001, and I'm beaming in my cap and gown. I'm a proud HBCU GRAD! Having my cousin give the commencement speech was the icing on the cake. The part of his speech that sticks in my head was when he said, *"I know we have those graduating Magna Cum Laude and Summa Cum Laude, but this is for those who are graduating "Thank You, Laude!"* I felt that in my **sha-na-na eboshada**, so much so I jumped up like I was in church, doing my praise wave and yelling, "Say that!" He was preaching! Best college speech EVER!!!

Degree presentations were underway, and my stomach was doing flips, waiting for my row to get in line. It wasn't nerves causing the butterflies in my stomach; it was the excitement of finally achieving a goal I'd been working so long and hard for. When it was my turn, and my name was called, the open football stadium was filled with screaming and cheering from my family. They were so incredibly proud. Everyone was waiting for me at the back of the stadium to continue the "love fest," showering me with congratulatory hugs, balloons, and flowers. Jackson was in the front, ready with a big hug and beautiful flowers. It was the cherry on top of my "graduation sundae!"

After many pictures and a few joyous tears, we started saying our goodbyes in a rush to get to Winston-Salem for my cousin's wedding, where I would be singing. I was okay with not having the typical after-graduation celebration party like most. It was a family affair, and everyone who knows me knows it's family above everything. So, I kissed my grandma, Dad, Stepmom, and brothers before heading to our next destination. My mom, stepfather, and sisters went ahead; Jackson and I weren't far behind. We had packed my car up the night before because I had moved out of my apartment and said goodbye to Durham…my home away from home and safe haven for five years. I'm not going to lie; it made me a bit emotional. But there was no time to cry; we had places to go, people to see, and a wedding to attend. Thankfully, we made it to Winston in time to change and not be late for the festivities.

This day was a gift that would keep on giving. I was so over the moon that my dream of earning my degree had finally come to fruition. Now, I'd have the honor of singing at my cousin's wedding in front of Jackson and a large portion of my relatives. This would be the first time Jackson would hear me sing and meet this side of my family... and oh boy, them Mackeys were the TRUTH!

I was anxious to see how the family intros would go since my uncles didn't hold any punches, especially my uncle, Earnest, who was my singing partner and had nicknamed me 'Bird.' He was a very tall man with a voice like silk and massive hands of iron. Like his voice, his hands lived up to their reputation—soft but strong; he was the ultimate protector. He saw Jackson sitting beside me, and before I could introduce them, Uncle Earnest blurted out, "So, I hear you from New Jersey." We weren't sure if it was a question or a comment to let Jackson know that he had already been "briefed" on who he was. Clearly, my mom had already provided some background information. It was officially on! I hoped Jackson was braced for this impending interrogation.

Despite my concerns, Jackson was unshaken and stood to greet my uncle with a handshake, only to be left hanging. Recognizing my uncle's attempt to be intimidating, Jackson responded, "Yeah," with a new bass in his voice. This was viewed as an act of "aggression" (not really) and further fueled my uncle's desire to continue the harassment of my boyfriend. Uncle Earnest stepped even closer to Jackson (and he was already uncomfortably close), then looked him up and down with an unsettling snarl on his face. Trying to hold in my laughter, I sat back and watched it all unfold. "I don't know you," Uncle Earnest growled. He didn't give Jackson a chance to respond before he barked with a little more volume, "You think you big, don't you?! That don't mean anything nigga, I'll knock you out!" Jackson looked over at me in shock or fear, not sure which, prompting my uncle to continue his rant, asking, "Why are you looking at her? She can't save you! Look at me; I'm talking to you!" Stepping in closer, Uncle Earnest, almost 7 feet tall, hovered over Jackson like an umbrella. It almost appeared as if Jackson attempted to stand on his toes to reduce the intimidation factor. It was like Dwayne Johnson meets Kevin Hart; I even recall my Uncle saying, "I ought to punch you on the top of your head! Listen here, you hurt my niece, and I'll kill you. No questions asked!" Still, without cracking a smile, Uncle Earnest reached down, grabbed the hand that Jackson had extended earlier, and gave it a firm shake. It was not out of respect, but was his way of guaranteeing his threat! Then he walked over to me, kissed me on the cheek while giving Jackson a final side-eye, and walked off. "Whew, he's intense," Jackson mumbled while looking around to ensure he was gone. "Nah, but he meant what he said," I responded, dying laughing on the inside. I'm pretty sure my uncle was on the other side of the room laughing and telling the rest of my uncles how he scared the piss outta my boyfriend. Boy, the comedy of it all…gotta love it!!

After the reception, we went back to my mom's house and got out of our wedding clothes. Jackson helped me unload and store my stuff in my mom's garage so we could finally kick back and unwind from such a fantastic day. At least, that was my plan. But Jackson had something else on his mind. While downstairs, out of the blue, he asked me when I was moving to Jersey. I didn't want to have this conversation right now, but to prevent sparking an argument, I told him it depended on my law school admission test (LSAT) results, which I was scheduled to take in a month. The school I was accepted into (Rutgers, Seton Hall, or now Alma mater, and my first choice, NCCU) would also be a determining factor. It was already understood that if I got back into Central, I wasn't moving; a fact that he wasn't ready to accept. Despite how hard I wanted to avoid it, Jackson tried to turn it into an argument by suggesting I was only stringing him along. As calmly as I could, I reminded him that he had always known my plans and was free to leave this relationship if, at any time, it wasn't fulfilling his needs. That's where it started going downhill.

Jackson's pity party was messing with my "happy high!" He even accused me of not caring or loving him, which was far from the truth. It's not that I didn't love Jackson; I had deep feelings for him. He was perfect. He checked all the boxes. I'd prayed about him...about us...and envisioned us being married and having our own family. Maybe he sensed my recent hesitation due to his sporadic mood changes and was concerned. Perhaps it was the fact that, because of past experiences and my share of disappointments, I was overly independent. I was definitely not "the princess who needed a prince to come and save her" type. But I made that clear upfront. So, who knows what sparked this Jekyll & Hyde moment, but I was not in the mood...not today.

The day was coming to an end, and I hadn't even had time to take it all in. I am a college graduate! I made it through! And next up was law school! Both physically and now mentally exhausted, the only words I could muster as I felt myself dozing off was, "Thank You, Lord!"

Sunday morning came before my body had time to really rest. Jackson got up early and headed back to NJ. My mom and stepfather were also leaving to go on a quick getaway to the beach. So, it was just me and my little sister for the week while they were away. It was nice to be able to sleep and not have to worry about a class schedule or homework. I didn't mind that I had to get up early every day to help my little sister get ready for school. I would prepare her breakfast and lunch, go back to sleep after she left, and sleep uninterrupted for hours. I was making up for all the rest I had missed out on for years! It was great!

13

LOST AND *Not* FOUND

◆

It was Sunday afternoon; the week seemed to fly by so fast. My mom and stepfather were back from the beach. When she came through the door, I was a bit taken aback to see that she was walking with a noticeable limp. Since neither of them volunteered any information, I followed her down the hall and into their room, looking for answers about what happened to her leg. She sat on the bed but still did not respond to my inquiry. I was not accepting her silence, so I asked again. Still no response. I turned and looked at my stepfather, who had come into the room and sat in the chair on the opposite side of the bedroom. By this time, I was not sure what to think and was trying not to draw my own conclusion, so I stood there, turning my head back and forth between them, waiting for a response. After about a minute, my mom spoke up, rather nonchalantly, saying, "I have had this limp for a bit. I went to the doctor a while back because it would come and go, but it wasn't getting any better. So, the doctor ran some tests." As I stood in the doorway, I waited for some sign from my mom; a tear, crack in her voice…something that would help me better gauge this situation. But she gave me nothing. She was calm, never changed the tone of her voice, and maintained eye contact with me the entire time. I turned and looked at my stepfather, who had completely turned away and was facing their bathroom. I was officially about to blow! The room was eerily silent, but my face was screaming, "ONE OF Y'ALL BETTER TELL ME WHAT'S GOING ON!!" and they both knew it. "I have Cancer," my mom suddenly whispered. Wait what? Did I honestly hear those words come from **my** mother's mouth? No! No! No! Not my mother. There's no way that's what she said. I quickly turned to face her and saw the tears fall from her eyes with a blank stare as if she were talking to a stranger. I couldn't move; my feet suddenly felt heavy. I immediately had an overwhelming feeling to scream, but no sounds would come out of my mouth. My head started to spin as my emotions overloaded. I kept saying to myself, "Cancer? Are you kidding me?! My Mother?" I knew and saw cancer's impact from a distance, but now here it was in our home, up close and personal. Processing this was a gut punch, and I instantly realized why I couldn't cry... I was too pissed off!!

When life comes at you fast, supernatural strength kicks in. In this very minute, for this particular person, at this crucial moment in her life, I had to be the strong one. I had to move into her role and let her know it was okay for her to move into mine. I knelt down in front of my mom, wrapped my arms around her, and hugged her tight. After a few moments in our embrace, I felt her body relax; she leaned into me and took a breath. It was as if the weight of being "everything for everybody" lifted from her shoulders, and she realized she could be vulnerable and trust that things would be alright. That's when the floodgate of emotions opened. I whispered, "I got you, Mom," as we wiped away the tears. She never doubted me, and I was determined not to disappoint her. If it was a fight cancer wanted, it was a fight it would get. Ring the bell...

In the days following my mom's diagnosis, she tried to prepare herself to tell my sisters and brother. She told my brother and asked me to be with her when she called my oldest sister. She couldn't bear to share the news with my baby sister, who was 11 years old (her birthday was right around the corner), so my oldest sister and I took on that task for her. It was so hard to look into those innocent eyes and tell her that Mom was battling for her life, but it had to be done.

In an effort to maintain some normalcy, my family decided to go out for the afternoon to the movies and then to dinner. This was the perfect time for me to call Jackson and tell him about my mom's diagnosis. I was finally home alone and figured this would be my only opportunity to cry all I wanted on my man's shoulder and be comforted and reassured that everything would be alright. I called him but almost instantly felt uneasy about talking to him about what was happening. Maybe it was me not wanting to speak her diagnosis out loud or give it credence because doing so, in my opinion, was the same as accepting it, and I wasn't fully ready to do that. I was banking on Jackson "talking me off the bridge," but I got the opposite...I got silence. He was quiet as a mouse. Not a "there, there," a "it's going be okay baby," or a "I'm praying for y'all." NOTHING!! I was an emotional mess, and he couldn't muster up not one comforting word for his girlfriend, who had recently found out her mother had cancer. Instead, he had the nerve to ask why I was crying. That was the last straw for me. Without another word, I hung up and refused to answer his calls the rest of the day. I was in total disbelief that Jackson was completely incapable of showing an ounce of compassion to the person he was supposed to love. I was done...you could stick a fork in me because I WAS DONE!

In the days following, thoughts of my mom and her cancer diagnosis, my little sister, and a million other things ran loose and untamed in my head like a pack of wild horses. I continued not to answer Jackson's calls, as I was still dumbfounded by his lack of care at a moment when I really needed him. "Guess it's just you and me, Lord," I said under my breath as I stared off into space.

"I'm not quite sure how we got here, but I'm thinking that some of that supernatural strength would be pretty helpful right now. I'd really appreciate it. Thanks."

Without a doubt, He was the only one I would be able to rely on from here on out.

14

CHECK *Please!*

The mental fog was still hanging over me; I couldn't shake it. My mom's first treatment had been scheduled, and although I held it together in front of her, I wasn't handling it well. It was clear that I needed to get away and try to clear my head a bit.

Jackson and I hadn't seen each other since my graduation, and we hadn't talked since I hung up on him after telling him about Mom's cancer. But right about the time when I felt like my "cup runneth over," he called and apologized for how our last conversation ended. Jackson explained that although he understood why I was crying, he really didn't know what he could've or should've said that would bring me comfort at that moment. He then offered me time away from everything as a peace offering. So, I took him up on his offer; he was a good distraction. I decided to take a few days before we started Mom's chemo journey. It was a much-needed break.

As I exited the plane, I saw Jackson there waiting for me. We made eye contact, but he seemed hesitant to move in my direction, as if he was unsure how to approach me. Our walk to the parking lot was quiet, and we rode in complete silence, which didn't sit right with me; it triggered my anxiety (like I didn't have enough on my mind). The drive to Jackson's condo from the airport felt like it took forever. Once there, he went into the bedroom, leaving me in the living room again, in silence. This was not what I anticipated when I talked to him about coming to visit. I could have stayed at home for this. I finally got up to see what the deal was with him. He was sitting in the room like I wasn't there. I cleared my throat to announce my presence, and when he looked up, he said softly, "Hey, I ran you a bath." Oh okay. I had it all wrong. He left me in the living room to get things ready for **us** to spend some quality time together, starting with a bath.

My mood instantly went from sad to giddy. However, that feeling didn't last long. Before I could verbalize my appreciation, Jackson got up and left the room. I was confused and once again alone and in silence. I never considered an alternative to explain Jackson's interaction with me. Maybe the awkwardness was Jackson being in unfamiliar territory and not knowing what to say. Or it could have been me being extra sensitive because of what was going on with my mom. Either way, I didn't even have the energy to ask for an explanation. It was going to be what it was going to be.

I was so mentally and physically exhausted. A long hot bath was exactly what I needed. As I got into the bubble-filled water, my body seemed to collapse from the weight of my emotions. I barely had the strength to keep my head above the water. I screamed and cried, and the longer I sat there, the harder I cried, and the more tears fell. I was so drained. I hoped the bath would wash away my feelings, but that was wishful thinking. I woke the following day determined not to succumb to the pain. As usual, Jackson had gotten up early, worked out, showered, dressed, and was cooking breakfast by the time I came into the kitchen. "You want to eat?" He asked. "Yes," I responded. Jackson put a beautifully made plate on the table in front of me and then sat on the other side with his plate...in silence. After breakfast, I mentioned that I wanted to ride the motorcycle, so he asked me to grab both helmets and meet him out front. He knew that the bike was my happy place. It was peaceful and freeing; I loved everything about it. We rode out with no particular destination in mind and no pre-planned agenda. We were just riding. We cruised for hours before stopping for lunch.

The deafening silence continued. The random small talk wasn't productive, and it seemed like Jackson had something to ask me but was struggling to get it out. I had no idea what he had to say, but clearly, it was the main thing on his mind. Then, out of nowhere, he blurts out, "Will I lose you?" I almost choked on my food. "Lose me?" I responded. "What do you mean, Jackson? Where did that come from?" He glanced up from eating and said, "You can't be thinking about us anymore with what is happening with your mom." I immediately lost my appetite. "You're right. I'm not thinking about us or what will become of us right now! Sorry." I answered with my annoyance on full display. "I know that might not be what you wanted to hear, Jackson," I continued, trying to reel my attitude back in, "But that's all I have right now. I know it's not fair, but it's all I got." I was foolish to think that the directness of my response would shut this uncomfortable conversation down…the question kept coming. "So, is this a kiss-off weekend?" he asked, looking a bit puzzled and slightly angry. "It doesn't have to be, Jackson," I replied softly, "but I can't make any promises right now." He nodded as if to acknowledge our relationship's apparent uncertainty, then looked down at his plate and pretended to finish his food. I had hoped that the open possibilities that my response presented would help salvage our lunch date, but I guess that was too much to ask.

We finished lunch and headed back to the condo. The mood had changed. Jackson was noticeably agitated, and I was a little perturbed myself. I'm sorry I couldn't give him any definitive answers, but why would he think I could…especially now? I was irritated that his entire line of questioning seemed to be his way of making me choose, but again, why, especially now, would he think I could or would? Better yet, why would he want me to? It made no sense. I couldn't wrap my mind around any of it and wasn't in the mood to try. I jumped in the shower, hoping to clear my head and give each of us time to cool down. As I came out of the bathroom, I noticed Jackson sitting on the floor up against the bed. To clear the air and put the uncomfortableness of the afternoon behind us, I suggested we spend the evening in Hoboken. Jackson agreed and went to get dressed so we could go and enjoy a great night out on the town. Hoboken, here we come!

15

Sing LIKE I TAUGHT YOU, TINA

There was always something going on in Hoboken. Jackson and I often hung out there when I would visit. We decided to hang out at a popular bar cluster in the area. As we got closer, we saw an outside event going on and decided to be a part of the scene. A wooden chalkboard was posted outside the buildings with the words 'OPEN MIC NIGHT' written big and bold in colorful chalk. OMG! This was what I needed, which also must have been true for the other patrons clambering to add their names to the open mic list as well. I was so excited because singing was my sanctuary, and doing it in front of strangers was less unnerving because they generally gave authentic responses. So, since I've always found solace in bellowing out a tune or two (it was my therapy), I didn't hesitate to find comfort in the mic whenever the opportunity presented itself.

Jackson retreated inside one of the bars to get us some drinks while I grabbed an unoccupied bar table in the courtyard. Not far from our spot, the DJ started setting up the speakers, the screen, and the mics in preparation for the festivities. The open mic sign-up sheet was on one of the tables off to the side, and the black song binders were randomly placed on tables around the venue. I was perusing through one of the binders when Jackson returned with our drinks. "You going to sing?" Jackson asked with concern on his face. "Absolutely!" I responded quickly. It was my happy place, so why not?

A couple of drinks later, the open mic event was in full swing. My turn hadn't come around yet, but it was okay. I was patient. The atmosphere was lively and entertaining. I was fully engrossed in watching the different patrons show off their vocal skills. Some were amazing, while others were more on the humorous side. The drinks were excellent. And although we didn't have high hopes for the food, that was even good; a great addition to the fantastic entertainment. The night was intoxicating, and I hadn't been on the mic yet. We also enjoyed "people-watching" while we waited for the DJ to call my name. Looking around, I noticed a familiar face at a nearby table. I tapped Jackson's arm and said, "I see someone I know. I'm going over to say hello." He looked at me, slightly confused, then responded, "Oh, OK." But as I was about to head over that way, I heard, "Next up to the mic, we have Victoria."

I stopped in my tracks, did an about-face, and made a beeline to the stage. Once in position, I looked out into the crowd and saw Jackson beaming with pride. His bright smile fueled my fire. I was ready to do my thang! I grabbed the mic, and as soon as the instrumental intro started, the audience was in disbelief that I was going to attempt one of Whitney Houston's greatest hits. I began to sing with my eyes fixed directly on Jackson. *'I know that when you look at me, there's so much that you just don't see, but if you would only take the time, I know in my heart, you'll find. A girl who's scared of something, who isn't always strong...'* I wasn't sure if he could decipher all of the lyrics because of the crowd noise, but I hoped he did. As I came to the climax of the song, I scanned the room to better engage with the crowd and noticed the same familiar face in the crowd looking dead at me. Acknowledging his presence, I smiled and got ready to close this performance out with a bang. Belting out the last note, I could hardly hear the instrumental over the applause, the whistling, the yelping, and the DJ hyping it up, saying, "Whew y'all! This girl got some skills! Give it up one more time for soulful singer Victoria!" The DJ's new nickname for me reignited the crowd's cheers, and as I headed back to my table, they let me know how much they enjoyed my performance. The compliments from fellow patrons and performers were coming from every direction. Although it was a bit overwhelming initially, it was a moment I'd never forget!

As I pushed my way through the mass of people to reach my table, that familiar face made his way to me and greeted me with the biggest hug. "What are you doing here?" he asked. "What am *I* doing here? The better question is, what are *you* doing here?" I responded jokingly. He walked with me to where Jackson was still sitting. "JACKSON!" I screamed at the top of my lungs. At first, it was because I was so excited, but then I realized I needed to hit another octave just so he could hear me over the noise. "This is my cousin, William. William, this is my boyfriend, Jackson." William extended his hand to greet Jackson and said, "Nice to meet you." "Likewise," Jackson responded less enthusiastically. "I see you still singing," William says. "Of course! You know me!" I answered, smiling, still giddy from my performance.

As we stood there laughing, a female walked up to the table and let William know she was ready to go. William turns and quickly introduces her to me and Jackson. She waved and complimented me on my singing. I thanked her and turned to William, "Now I see why you're in Jersey, cuz!" Laughing and blushing, he responded, "I'm tryin' to be like you!" After a little more chit-chat and laughter, we exchanged another big hug before he and his friend turned to leave. "Well, it was good to see you," he says, still seemingly surprised to have run into me here, of all places. While walking away, he turned around again, waved goodbye, and said, "Call me tomorrow; maybe we can hang out before you leave." Waving back, I smiled with joy at how great it was to see William and how amazing the night was going. I hadn't had this much fun in what felt like an eternity. But I should have known that it would be short-lived. Jackson couldn't wait until William and his friend were far enough from us to ask, "Your cousin on whose side?" "My mom," I replied carelessly, still bopping my head to the music blasting in the courtyard. "Why didn't he ask about your mom?" Jackson continued. I immediately noticed the accusatory nature of Jackson's questions and tried my best to set the record straight and nip this conversation in the bud before it got out of hand. However, before I could do that, a random guy came up to the table, visibly intoxicated, saying, "You totally rocked that song! You have a beautiful voice. Sing again, for me." Jackson, with his funky attitude, didn't give me a chance to respond. He looked at the guy and said, "Nah, bruh; she done entertaining tonight!" We all know that alcohol and attitude make for unfavorable conditions, and that's what was brewing here. The random guy laughs and says, "Who you, her manager?". Jackson didn't find that as funny as he did and became even more aggravated than before. I wasn't sure if he was irritated by the compliments from the random guy or his self-inflicted assumptions about who William was, but in the blink of an eye,

Jackson jumped up, grabbed the guy by his shirt, and lifted him off the ground. I was so caught off guard that I started yelling at Jackson to put the guy down. He eventually let him go, and needless to say, that was the end of our wonderful evening. I was in disbelief as I walked away to get in the truck. When Jackson came walking towards me, I saw red. Before he could open his mouth, I screamed to the top of my lungs, "What the hell is wrong with you? You out here picking a fight with some random dude for what? Are you that insecure?" He was oblivious to why I was so angry and didn't see any reason why he needed to apologize. His only focus was knowing the truth about William. He kept saying, "Tell me the truth. William isn't your cousin; he's an ex, isn't he?" He refused to apologize, so I refused to respond to his asinine questions and accusations. You would think my silence was a clue that the discussion was over for me. But it wasn't. During the entire ride back, Jackson continued asking the same questions. Even after we returned to his place, he wouldn't let up, and I had all I could take. Unable to maintain my composure, I turned and screamed, "What the fuck does it matter? I told you who he was when I introduced you, and you evidently don't believe me. I'm tired, and I'm done talking about this shit. So, I hope your back is strong; you'll need it sleeping on that couch tonight!" I slammed the bedroom door, hoping the impact would take it off its hinges. ruly this shit was for the birds, and my name wasn't Tweety!

16

Shattered BEYOND REPAIR

◆

A nightmare... You know the ones where you're trying to scream and you can't; you're trying to move, but there's a weight so heavy you can't push it off, and all you want to do is wake up? Then, when you finally wake up, you are sweating, out of breath, and a bit spooked. I thought that was what I was experiencing, but when I was jolted out of my sleep by Jackson's hand over my mouth, I quickly knew this was real. He was drunk. I could smell the liquor on his breath. As I fought to move his hand from my mouth, he pushed down even harder. He pulled up my satin nightgown and threw my legs back over my shoulders. His entire body weight pressed against my body, forcing my knees into my chest. I struggled against his weight to get loose, but I was clearly fighting a losing battle. He rips my underwear off and enters me anally; each thrust more forceful and painful. My muffled screams got louder and louder. He then enters me vaginally. His grip got tighter and tighter. I was paralyzed. His ejaculation was so intense he was shaking. It weakened him to the point I thought I could overpower him and get loose, but I still couldn't move. He finally released his hold of my legs and removed his hand from my mouth. Then, like nothing had happened, he got up and walked out of the room. I tried to scream, but nothing came out. He had stolen my voice and so much more. I was devastated.

Scared to move or even breathe, the tears begin to flow. I sat up in the bed, hugging my knees, trying to process the horror that I had just experienced. My mind was spinning like a top. I was in complete shock. Even after several minutes, I still could not move, but I knew I needed to. Fear had completely taken over. I was alone, too far from home to call anyone, and terrified he would hear me. It was hopeless...I was trapped.

I sat on the bed in sheer panic, wondering how I was going to get out of there. This was a life-or-death situation; either his or mine, and I wasn't planning on dying today. I couldn't sit here and let him hold me hostage in this room. I HAD TO MOVE...NOW! So, I slowly and carefully crawled off the bed, scared he would come back and the nightmare would start all over again. I strategically placed my feet on the hardwood floor, quickly gathered my bags, and threw on some pants and a shirt over my nightgown. I cautiously walked through the doorway and into the living room, praying the whole time that the cracking of the floorboards wouldn't alert him to my movements.

My heart began to pump harder when I didn't see Jackson anywhere. It was as if it was about to bust out my chest. I froze. I knew his condo wasn't that big. Was he in the bathroom? Was he behind me? Was he waiting for me on the other side of the door? I started to panic; then, I heard a moan. I looked in that direction and saw him passed out on the couch. I had to get out now! I tried to move my feet, but again, they wouldn't move. I looked back towards the couch and back at the door. "I need to get to the door without him waking up," was all I could think. The tears were flowing so hard that my vision was blurred. I could barely see the door but knew this next move would decide my fate. I took a deep breath and took two of the biggest steps my 5 foot, 3-and-a-half-inch height would afford me. Thankfully, the alarm was off. I quietly unlocked the door and slowly turned the knob, praying that my efforts would not be in vain. Once on the other side of the door, I positioned my bag so that it would stop the door from slamming. I was out!

I ran to the elevator, frantically pushing the button to go down. It felt like it took forever for the doors to open. When I got to the lobby, I sprinted outside, desperately hailing a cab. A couple of them were always staged at the end of the corners. I spotted one at the end of the block and walked quickly towards it. At the time, I hadn't even noticed that I never put on my shoes. But oh well...

Still in disbelief, I took a few minutes to breathe, then pulled a pair of flip-flops out of my bag as the cab driver pulled up. I quickly hopped in. "Newark Airport, please," I stuttered. Then I grabbed my phone to make flight arrangements. "I need to fly out on the next flight to Charlotte, NC," I told the airline agent. Ironically, I was grateful for the open ticket Jackson purchased. I was going home.

The flight home was rough. I don't remember breathing until I touched down in NC. I had so many emotions running through me. When I pulled up to my mom's house, she and my little sister were headed to church. "You're back early," she said, walking past me to her car. "Yes, ma'am," I replied, trying to smile and not alert her that anything was wrong. I noticed that my stepfather's car wasn't in the driveway, which meant he had already left for work. I was home alone. I dropped my bag at my bedroom door and walked to the bathroom; I turned on the shower and stepped into the tub. As soon as the water hit my skin, I screamed!

Every part of me (mind, body, and spirit) began to feel the assault...the rape. OH MY GOD JACKSON RAPED ME! I felt like I was drowning. I had suddenly come out of complete survival mode, and the realization of what happened was starting to sink in. How did I get here? What did I do? I wanted to pinch myself to be sure this wasn't a dream. It wasn't…this was a nightmare, and I so desperately wanted to wake up!

The sound of my little sister yelling my name through the house instantly pulled me out of the "trance" I had fallen into while standing in the shower. I was just watching the beads of water roll off my skin like marbles. I didn't even realize how long I was in there. I tried to regain my composure and force another smile on my face before I emerged from the bathroom. It was a physical and emotional feat to hide noticeable bruises from my mom, who definitely didn't need anything else to worry about. She was noticeably drained already. She was preparing to be admitted into the hospital in a couple of days to start her cancer treatment. There was no way I was going to add to her stress, although what I really wanted right now was for my mom to wrap her arms around me and tell me that everything would be ok. But since that wasn't possible, I decided to push the pain down to the deepest and darkest places of my being for the greater good of those I love. I only needed to focus on what was in front of me: my mom and sister. I continued to remind myself that I was home safe and would never see him again because we were done! And if he EVER showed his face here, he'd better be prepared to die…because he would. I'd make sure of it!

The doctors had been in and out of Mom's room all morning, checking her vitals and explaining everything about her treatment to us. I was suffering from risk overload seeing the giant bags of "poison" (experimental drugs) that hung over her bed and were connected to her. But I was in a zone and focused. She was the center of my life now. My days were spent at the hospital, and at night, I went home. My phone had been turned off, and I hadn't really thought about turning it back on because I knew Jackson had called and probably was still calling. While trying to hide from him, I had shut myself off from everyone else. How had he managed to rob me of my freedom and dictate my interactions from afar? I had already given up part of my life to care for my mom, who deserved my full attention. I would no longer allow Jackson to occupy any more space in my universe. He had already stolen so much. I needed to take my power back... I turned my phone back on.

There were messages galore. I didn't bother to listen or reply to any from Jackson, and there were plenty. But I didn't erase them either. I wasn't sure why I felt that I couldn't, but I was convinced it was linked to the trauma I experienced at his hands. I still haven't thought it all through yet. I was still in the processing phase. One night after my mom's treatment, my stepfather called to let me know that she was not doing very well. The doctors weren't sure she would make it through the night. She wasn't as responsive to the chemotherapy as they would have liked, leading them to put her in a drug-induced coma. I didn't know what to do. I didn't have anyone to call or confide in. I HAD NO ONE! I felt as if I had reached my breaking point. I was an emotional wreck!

17

NO PIECES TO *Pick Up*

◆

School was back in session, and I was home with my little sister, playing the role of Mom. It was nothing easy about this, but I had to suck it up and do what needed to be done. I found myself crying a lot. I felt so helpless, alone, and angry on so many levels and for so many different reasons; helpless because I could not defend myself, so how was I supposed to protect my sister? Alone because I couldn't confide in anyone...no one would understand what I was going through; angry because my mom was fighting for her life; angry that the one person I thought I could find refuge in violated me, mind, body, and soul; angry because this was my fault. I must have missed the signs. And I'm furious because, for some foolish reason, I was now keeping a secret that haunted me with every breath I took. I was suffering in silence, and the only one who knew was God. And Oh, I was furious with Him too! I blamed Him for allowing it all to happen; every single fucking thing! This was the very moment I stopped talking to Him. I no longer had the words to say. And in such a broken state, I didn't realize my words were overrated in God's eyes. He wanted my heart, but I was too scared to relinquish it again. Sad but true.

When Mom got home, things were different. She was different; I was different; Life for our family, as we knew it, was different. I was now her full-time nurse. My stepfather had emotionally and physically detached from the situation. It had become too much for him. In real-time, I witnessed the wedding vows *'through sickness and health'* fall by the wayside. He went as far as to move into the basement full-time and was only seen when he came upstairs to shower. Not only was he abandoning my mom, but also my little sister, his biological child. I didn't have the emotional capacity to dissect that and help my little sister understand why, all of a sudden, her father seemingly wanted to have nothing to do with her and our mom...his wife. I wanted to kill him for being so selfish!

The truth of the matter was I would have to do this on my own, for real. The saving grace was that I was determined not to let my mom down. So, step one was to make sure I ran her home like a well-oiled machine. I made sure all her and my baby sister's needs were met. I was her personal assistant, RN, stylist, chef, and physical therapist, all wrapped in one. Despite all the hell we sheltered her from, my sweet sister found so much joy in being my little CNA helper. It seemed to give her purpose and me a much-needed helping hand.

The morning routine was well underway. I had breakfast for my mom and sister warming on the stove, school forms were signed, bookbag and lunch were packed, and medication was ready to distribute. I was in my zone until the house phone rang and stopped my progress. "Hello," I answered. To my surprise, it was my stepfather calling from work (a rarity), "Victoria, turn on the TV," he said in a panic. I didn't hesitate or ask any questions. I grabbed the remote, wondering what could possibly be happening in Winston-Salem this early morning that was so urgent and had my stepfather so distressed. When I looked at the screen, all I saw was smoke coming from a sky-rise building that looked very familiar. After a few seconds, it hit me. One of the Twin Towers in New York was on fire. I hadn't read the news feed at the bottom of the screen, so I wasn't sure what to make of what I was looking at. So I asked my stepfather, who was still on the phone, what was going on, and before he could respond, I saw a plane fly into the second building! "Oh My God!" I screamed, utterly shocked at what I was witnessing. I immediately asked him if this was a movie. He responded with even more emotion, "No!! We're under attack!" I stood frozen, staring at the TV; I couldn't even move my feet. Hearing my stepfather calling my name through the phone snapped me out of the instantaneous trance that the tragic scene had put me in. "Victoria! Victoria!" my stepfather screamed. "Didn't you say Jackson worked in the World Trade Center?" he asked with concern. In shock at what was happening, I hadn't even considered him or his well-being. "His building is beside the World Trade," I responded slowly. I immediately start praying for the thousands who lost their lives, their grieving families, the city of New York, and the United States as a whole. But one person was purposefully left out. I noticed the numb feeling that came over me when I heard my stepfather say his name. Inwardly, I hoped that he, by some slim chance, was a non-surviving victim of this horrible situation. Yeah, I know it was a vile and sinister thought, but my wounds were still fresh and wide open; I was still in agony and suffering daily. Although I kept it covered with the "band-aids of secrecy," trust and believe that with each passing day, the horror I experienced festered inside of me, poisoning every fiber of my being with each second I held it all in. Needless to say, I wasn't in a forgiving mood. I wouldn't have even poured water on him if he was lying at my feet, engulfed in flames. To me, it would be an appropriate judgment…karma, if you will…to what he did to me a couple of months ago. The *coup de grâce* would've been me singing "*Burn,*

Baby Burn" (Disco Inferno by The Trammps, 1976) as it took place.

Coup de grâce - [koo də 'gräs] a final blow or shot given to kill a wounded person or animal.

It wasn't a dream. The United States of America, the mightiest country in the world, had become victim to one of the most devasting terror attacks in history. The magnitude of what had happened stunned the world and left everyone old enough to see it unfold with memories they'd never forget. I screeched in horror, watching people on live TV jump from the burning towers. My intense reactions alarmed my mom so much that she shuffled down the hall, holding on to walls for balance, to come to check on me. We stood side by side in the kitchen, glued to the TV. With tears flowing down our cheeks, it was at that moment that our current situation seemed small compared to what we were witnessing. As one of the towers began to collapse, falling on what I knew to be the building that Jackson worked in, our inadvertent gasps and screams filled the room where we were now sitting. It all seemed unreal, despite the "in your face" evidence that this was happening in real-time, on national television, right before our eyes.

My thoughts went straight to Vincent, hoping and praying he wasn't in the midst of the chaos. Since all means of communication were down, my attempts to reach him via call and text were unsuccessful. Although everyone kept asking if I had heard from Jackson, I had yet to utter his name. My heart burned every time someone brought him up. They don't know how close I was to screaming, "Fuck that rapist; he deserves to die!" But I kept my composure and continued to give short answers or no answers at all. Again, he was none of my concern.

Over the next several days, it was like living in a real-life Groundhog Day movie. Every station had continued coverage of the tragedy. With each click of the remote, they played the events of 9/11 over and over as if the film was on repeat. It was beginning to be too much; it was emotionally draining. It didn't help that I still hadn't heard from Vincent. But as the thought left me, my phone rang. I didn't even look at the number nor hesitate to answer because I had been waiting to hear from Vincent; I knew it was him…it had to be him. "Hello," I quickly responded with so much anticipation. "So, you weren't going to call and check on me?" Jackson arrogantly replied. "No, but I see you're still alive," I responded while hanging up the phone. My heart was racing! I felt like I couldn't breathe. The anger and rage that rose up in me was dangerous, and I knew it. The sound of his voice brought about a level of anxiety that I had never felt before. To add insult to injury, he continued to call back. I wanted to throw the phone through the wall, but I didn't want to scare my mother, and I didn't want to break my phone and be unable to talk to Vincent when he called. Jackson remained persistent, calling regularly and leaving messages each time. He spoke more to my voicemail than he did to me when we were together.

Message one: *"So you leave without saying goodbye? Why? Clearly, I did or said something, but I'm not sure what it was that caused you to leave like that. Call me back so we can talk."* **Message two:** *"When I saw the blood on the sheets, I thought you just went to the store to get some tampons, but you never came back." What happened? Please call me back."* **Message three:** *"Everything is a blur; you know I blank out when I'm stressed. I can only see pieces. I guess I said or did something to you, but how will I know if you won't tell me what it was!?"* **Message four:** *"OK, since you won't answer my calls, I'm coming to see you; you do know I know where you live? I'll see you one way or the other!"* **Message five:** *"I can take a hint. Maybe I shouldn't come see you; I don't think I'll be welcomed."* **Message six:** *"I thought we would be able to talk this over. You clearly aren't mature enough to pick up the phone and have a conversation with me. So, you want to end it like this? Is* *this how you want things to end... unfinished? OK. You're going to regret it. Ok, we had an argument, and some things were said and done, but I didn't hurt you!"* It's funny how he wouldn't say on the voicemails what 'things' were done. Jackson was very calculating and careful with his words, almost like he didn't want to incriminate himself. Smart man...so smart he was stupid.

The harassment continued for a few more days before Jackson finally got the hint and stopped calling. Hopefully, his reign of terror (via my phone) was over, and I could go back to life as it was before I heard his smug voice. After watching the 9/11 attacks unfold, I was determined not to allow him to steal anything else from me! Life was too short!

I had to find out where 'Victoria' was hiding, pull her out, dust her off, and get back to being who God had created me to be. Was I still angry? Absolutely! But I was committed to taking it one day at a time, even if it meant repairing everything that was broken in me. This transformation would start by letting people know that we were no longer in a relationship, something I had been pretty quiet about sharing.

The first opportunity to set the record straight came when my stepfather walked into the kitchen while I was eating breakfast to ask if I had heard from Jackson yet. "No, but my voicemail has." I unintentionally snapped back. "Oh," he says with his eyebrows raised. "So, ummm, y'all not together anymore?" he gently asked, still fishing for information. Here was my chance to finally say it out loud. "Naw, not for some time now," I replied without looking up from my plate. I thought that would be the end of the conversation, but, to my surprise, my stepfather felt the need to share his feelings about Jackson now that he was no longer in the picture. As he pulled the chair out to sit down at the table with me, he mumbled, "Good. He seemed controlling to me, and he was wound too tight." I put my fork off to the side of my plate and leaned back in my chair, attitude dripping off me like sweat. "And you didn't think that was information worth sharing?' I responded, annunciating every syllable in each word. He paused before answering, possibly rethinking his decision to share his previous thoughts with me. "Now, Victoria," he started cautiously, "since when did you start listening to my opinion about someone you were dating?" There was a lot of truth in what he said, but it didn't change the fact that I, at this very moment, was feeling like a fire-breathing dragon, and he was 'bout to catch these flames!!! "You've never expressed your opinion," I replied as I pushed away from the table, "well, at least not to my face. So, it's whatever now." I dropped my plate in the sink on purpose (possibly adding a little extra force) so that he understood that I was irritated and done with this conversation. What he thought didn't matter then, and it sho' didn't matter in that moment.

SIDE NOTE: I didn't care about disrespecting my stepfather. He knew that when it came to my mom, I would kill him...I only needed a reason. And his actions and treatment of her when she needed him most gave me the green light I needed. Furthermore, adding his two cents was comical, especially seeing how he wasn't even honoring his vows right now. The only reason I wasn't choking the life out of him was because my little sister needed me. I couldn't abandon her like he was doing.

18

$\mathcal{Joy}$ COMETH IN THE MORNING?

◆

Despite the circumstances, I found my niche, and things were running smoothly. I was managing this game of life like Troy Polamalu, stopping the run and crushing dreams on the field. I finally felt in control. Being my mom's caregiver and raising my little sister had become second nature. They were now my reason for existing; I wouldn't have changed that for the world. I was so dialed in, making sure they were squared away, that I had not noticed we were almost halfway into a new year. That was the moment when my body notified me that I was exhausted. Although I didn't trust anyone to manage my mom's care, I knew I needed a break before I found myself too worn out to continue giving her the attention she needed and deserved. The rest of my family agreed, so it was settled. Me time, here I come!

I needed an escape, and there was no better place to escape than Myrtle Beach for Memorial Day weekend. A couple of my friends had been asking me to go with them, but I didn't think the timing would be right with the responsibilities I had taken on. On the other hand, this was the best time to get away and not think about anything except unwinding and having fun. And that's precisely what I planned to do. After making sure every detail was laid out for my mom and little sister, I picked up two of the six members of our Golden Girl Crew. It was officially a girls' trip; one that was well overdue. I didn't know how much I needed this until I realized how great it felt to be out of the house and be carefree, if only for a moment.

The drive down to the beach was only three hours. The closer we got to our destination, we could hear the bikes in the distance. It was like the atmosphere shifted, and our excitement intensified. We all agreed that finding something to eat would be first on our agenda before checking into our hotel. As we neared the strip, we stopped at Applebee's. It was obviously a fan favorite. From the parking lot to the inside of the restaurant, it was packed tight with a bunch of lively tourists and beachgoers. This was a sign of how things were going to go; it was a great way to start our weekend.

The atmosphere was jumping the whole time we were there. As we attempted to leave, a guy from one of the motorcycle groups that parked by my car reached out for my friend Lisa's hand and, real smooth-like, said, "You don't have to look no further; I'm right here!" Everyone, including the guys in his group, was so amused by his boldness that we all laughed. We were used to Lisa drawing a lot of attention everywhere we went because she was brick-house-built; blessed in all areas. She seemed intrigued, so she stopped to chat it up for a bit with her new friend while Ava and I waited by the car. After a few minutes, she walked over to us and said, "Come on, girls! We're going for a ride." The Golden Girl Crew's rule book states that no one rides anywhere alone at any time. If one goes, we all go; if we come together, we leave together. No exceptions. So, with the plan set, I went into the trunk to grab a pair of shorts to put under my sundress, then jumped in the backseat to slide them on while Ava and Lisa stood watch. It was a quick transition, and I emerged within seconds, ready to ride. Lisa walked over to "her guy" and got on his bike. Ava was already on her chosen bike, so it was my turn. But as I considered my options, Lisa yelled, "Victoria, you're going to ride with Trey." I nodded in agreement, but on my way over to his bike, I thought, 'Who the hell is Trey, and why am I feeling like I've been sold to the highest bidder?' But I took it all in stride, as I was committed to releasing my stress and enjoying this weekend. This bike ride was the key to getting my mind, body, and spirit where I needed them to be so I could fully immerse myself in this much-needed vacay.

Thankfully, it wasn't at all awkward. It turned out that Trey was the cousin of Lisa's guy, so he wanted to make sure that Trey wasn't left out. When I got closer to where he stood, he flashed me a smile but looked a bit concerned. With the introductions out of the way, he shyly asked if I was going to be comfortable riding in my sundress, which I thought was very gentlemanly of him. I kindly assured him I would be okay because this wasn't my first rodeo. "Ok. Well, I guess that's what I get for not minding my business," he responded, looking away as if embarrassed. We both laughed at the comments as we prepared to ride. Trey assured me he was a safe driver, quoting the famed tagline, "You're in good hands...like Allstate." I knew then that this was going to be fun.

Our ride was refreshing and right on time. Trey was funny and kept me laughing the whole time. We cut the trip with our new friends short because we had not yet checked into our rooms and didn't want to risk losing our reservation. So, they dropped us back at my car, which was still parked at Applebee's. Trey gave me his number and invited me to call him if I wanted to hang out again while we were here. Then, the girls and I jumped in the car and headed to our hotel. When we arrived, Lisa went inside to check us in while Ava and I unloaded the car. To make only one trip, I was trying to grab as many bags out of the car as possible when I heard Ava ask, "Victoria, isn't that Jackson?" I instantly felt sick to my stomach, angry, and nervous at the same time. When I looked up, low and behold, there he was, right in my line of sight. The only thought in my brain was, "Damn! Damn! Damn!" like Florida Evans' iconic scene on *Good Times*. I couldn't make myself invisible fast enough. He looked up from his conversation with his female passenger, seeming to peer in my direction. I prayed that he hadn't seen me. Again, "Damn! Damn! Damn!" In that heart-pounding moment, I remembered that I never told a soul that Jackon raped me, and like a ton of bricks, I was hit with the reality that no one but me, him, and God knew what happened.

Initially, I boxed my emotions up and pushed them to the side in the best interest of my mom and my little sister. But how was I going to handle this around friends? How was I supposed to keep it together? Seeing Jackson here, without warning, was triggering. I would have thought my chances of running into him again during Black Bike Week were really low. Obviously, I was wrong. With panic setting in, I screamed within myself, "WHERE THE HELL IS A GUN WHEN YOU NEED ONE?!" I quickly walked to the other side of the car, wondering if he saw me, praying that he didn't.

I was so flustered that I missed seeing Trey and his crew pull up. "What a coincidence this is," said the familiar voice that jarred me from my trance and franticness. I was able to pull myself together as best I could while the guys were dismounting their parked bikes. Thankfully, they were situated in a manner that blocked me from potential onlookers. "You're staying here too?" I asked, trying to hide my nervousness. "Yeah. What are the odds?" Trey responded, flashing his smile at me again. Feeling rescued, we continued our conversation while walking towards the hotel, not once looking back. Once in the lobby, Ava pulled me aside and asked, "So, what's up with you and Jackson?" I took a deep breath before answering, hoping to stop my heart from racing, and calmly responded, "Nothing anymore," with a blank look on my face that I hoped she would pick up on. She gave me a quick side-eye, then slowly walked away in the direction of the guy whose bike she rode on. I must have given a familiar look of concern or a cry for help with my eye, which had Ava on high alert. Thankfully, when she called on me for help, I was there to rescue her from the situation. Our unspoken communication acknowledged our commitment to having each other's back...no matter what.

Waking up in a hotel room that had a fantastic view, a bed with crisp white sheets, and no schedule to keep was everything I wanted and needed. I couldn't have asked for anything better...except breakfast. While out for breakfast, Ava, Lisa, and I tried to figure out what we were going to get into next. The sky was a beautiful baby blue, and the sun was kissing us in all the right places, so we decided to take the car back to the hotel and walk the strip. We weren't walking long before we were whisked away on bikes. After a few rounds of riding, I started feeling the effects of the heat and got really tired. The others agreed, so we caught rides back to the hotel to rest up until dinner. We soon realized how exhausted we were when "resting" turned into "napping." However, to our benefit, we woke up refreshed and ready to hit the strip again. On our way out, we ran into Trey and his crew on their way to dinner. Being the gentlemen that they were, they invited us to join them. Our evening was set, and we were not disappointed. The guys showed us a great time. Once back at the hotel, we realized how exhausted we truly were and couldn't wait to get to the room.

In the elevator, the girls and I recalled the highlights of our day and giggled over the conversations that were had in private as well as in public. The ding of the opening elevator door cued us to quiet down the laughter out of respect for others on our floor. Still, it was tough to contain the pleasure and excitement of enjoying our weekend so far. The doors opened, and we quietly continued the happy banter back and forth as we made our way to the room. When we turned the corner, the laughter stopped abruptly at the sight of Jackson standing just a few feet from our door. My heart started racing again, and like the last time, my only thought was, 'Damn! Damn! Damn!'

19

HANGING ON FOR *Dear* LIFE

I knew in my heart of hearts that the time would come when I would have to face the man who damaged me beyond repair and tried to destroy my life. But little did I know it would be here and now. By the way he was staring me and the girls down while we walked to the room, I thought to myself, "As much as I don't want to, I guess the time has come, so we 'bout to do this." The instantaneous look of concern on my face was a non-verbal indication to my friends that this was a high-alert situation. I stopped a few steps from the door, preparing to have one last conversation with Jackson. Lisa and Ava went straight into "protective sister" mode, asking if I wanted them to stay out there with me, then staring him down as they walked past him to get to our room. With where he stood compared to how close I was to our door, it didn't seem necessary that they stay in the hall since they were within earshot if I needed them. He also was very aware that I was loud enough to sound an alarm if it came to it.

He stood more than an arm's length away in silence, staring coldly at me. But I was not going to be intimidated, especially by him. I began to wonder how he knew where I was. Our room was registered under someone else's name, so how did he know what floor I was on? It suspiciously reminded me of my "encounter" with Jackson when we first arrived at the beach. It was an interesting coincidence that he was dropping off a female passenger in the parking lot of our hotel. My face must have been screaming my inner thoughts because Jackson broke his silence and said, "Surprised to see me?" Clearly, I was surprised, but I was not entertaining his foolishness. I wanted to know how he found me, but not enough to exchange more words than necessary.

Ignoring his question, I blurted out in frustration, "How did you know which floor I was on? Have you been following me?" He went back to his uncomfortable stare and silent treatment. I guess he was still trying to bully me, but I was having none of it...or so I thought. The hotel was usually loud and lively, full of people in and out at all times of the night. However, for some reason, it was noticeably quiet...too quiet. It was clear to me that this conversation, or a lack thereof, was going nowhere. I did not owe him anything, and it seemed like a waste of my time to continue standing there. He was still silent, and I was over it, so I began to walk toward my room. Before I knew it, Jackson grabbed me by my hair, pulled me back towards him, then put his hand around my neck and commenced to throw me up against the wall while choking me. I was so paralyzed with fear my body went limp. This was now a fight for my life. I gathered myself as best I could and began screaming and clawing and scratching at his hands to pry them from around my neck. I was trying to call for help but to no avail. He then threw me to the floor. I struggled to regain air, hoping to scream and yell for help again while crawling towards my room. But Jackson wasn't giving up. Before I could make it far, he grabbed me by my legs and pulled me further away from my room and further down the hallway. There was no way my friends would hear now. I was convinced that he wasn't going to stop until I was dead.

After dragging me to the end of the hall, Jackson lifted me off the ground by my hair and threw me over his shoulder as if I were a rag doll. I kept kicking and screaming for help, but there seemed to be no one around to hear me. I pounded on his back with my fist, but he continued walking to the end of the hallway near the balcony opening. I fought as hard as I could to get loose. When he got to the railing, he held me over the balcony by my ankles. My life flashed before me, and I started praying, "Father God, save me, rescue me!" I knew I wasn't going to make it out of this one. He was definitely going to let go. All of a sudden, I felt like I was being lifted from over the balcony, and the force threw me back onto the floor. I landed on my butt, and when I looked up, Jackson was walking back towards me. He then stopped in his tracks as if something or someone had spooked him, but no one was in the hallway. We were alone, or so I thought. I struggled to get on my feet and get to my room as quickly as I could before he got a second wind. As I got closer to our door, I heard another door open and saw one of the hotel guests peeking his head out to see what was going on. By then, I was close enough to bang on our door to alert Ava and Lisa. Ava opened the door, and she saw me in complete distress. All I uttered was, "Jackson." As if someone had shot her from a cannon, she ran down the hall looking for him while Lisa helped me into the room.

When she got me to the couch, Lisa grabbed her phone to call the police. Before they arrived, Ava returned to the room even more angry than before. She said she tried to get the security guards to apprehend Jackson, who was hiding in the bushes by the hotel until the police got there. Sadly, she couldn't convince them to help her. Lisa was noticeably shaken by what had gone unheard and unnoticed right outside our door. She angrily paced back and forth in the room, seemingly trying to calm herself down. "Why didn't you yell for help?" she asked frantically. "I *was* yelling and screaming. I can't believe y'all didn't hear me," I whispered, trying to catch my breath and shake off the feeling of his hand around my neck. "We only heard mumbles, like y'all were outside talking. I swear we didn't hear you screaming. You know we would have been right there!" Lisa explained with tears filling her eyes.

The police finally showed up, later than sooner, rolling about ten officers deep, and all of the Caucasian persuasion, except one. I knew from the start this was not going to go well. Showing zero compassion or empathy, one of the officers began asking us about what had happened. Despite the trauma, I gave him a very detailed account of the abuse I suffered only minutes before their arrival. However, I assumed from the questions that followed that this "band of merry men" didn't find my account of the events credible. "Ma'am, are you sure he "*attacked*" you, and you're not saying this to get back at him because you're mad?" one of the officers had the audacity to ask. Are you kidding me right now?! Who says that at a time like this? See, this was a prime example of why women do not feel comfortable enough to report abuse. I knew this type of behavior existed, but I hoped that I wouldn't have to deal with it during one of the most devastating moments of my life. In disbelief that the officer could even part his lips to say that, I looked through the sea of brown and khaki uniforms for a pair of friendly eyes that could possibly salvage this interview, only to find none, not even from the ONE that was "brown (skin folk)" like me. Needless to say, things got progressively worse from there. I'd had enough from these people when the officer decided it was a good idea to say, "I mean, you don't look like you have been abused." Now, on top of all my other emotions, I could officially add *irritated and devalued* to that list. Without hesitation, I angrily responded, "So, Mr. Officer, let me get this right: you believe that since my face is not disfigured and blood isn't all over the place, there's no way I could have been abused? Is that what you're saying?" Of course, there was no response. With my head in my hands, I took a deep breath to brace myself for the next ignorant comment to fly, and dammit if they did not disappoint. After a few moments of chattering and mumbling from the crowd, I heard the officer insultingly ask, "Ma'am, do you even know who it was that attacked you?" I was done. This interaction was over…it had to be over, or I would be the one leaving in handcuffs.

Ava sensed my irritation and responded on my behalf, saying, "Yes! It was her ex-boyfriend!" Wanting to be done with this interaction, I interrupted Ava's explanation and calmly asked, "What information do you need; his phone number, social security number, his address in Jersey City, NJ, his parent's address, the license plate number for his truck or his bike; what…what do you want?" I tried to keep it together, but the longer this man stood in front of me, the more pissed off I got! But he wasn't done pouring salt in my wounds. "Well, ma'am," he started in a discouraging tone, "all I'm saying is that if you want to press charges, I have to call and wake a judge up at this hour, and by the time we get a warrant for his arrest, he could be halfway back to Jersey." Then why were they even here? Why was my room full of MEN (Keystone Cops, if you will) who only made me feel like I was being attacked all over again? I WAS SO DONE! Lisa, who rarely gets upset, blurts out, "This is such bullshit! What the hell are y'all good for? Did you hear her? She was attacked, and all you're concerned about is how much work you will have to do. Unbelievable!!!!" Seeing the tears falling from her eyes and understanding that nothing productive would come from this, I wiped my face, pushed myself up from the chair, and thanked the officers for nothing as I ushered them to the door. Ava came in from the balcony and handed me the phone. It was my mom. "Ma," was the only word I could utter before I broke down sobbing. Ava stood behind me, trying to hold me up, but I was like dead weight; my body had checked out. I could hear my mom on the phone saying, "Just come home, baby. Just come home."

20

THE MORNING *After*

T he sun at the beach always seemed so different from the sun in North Carolina. It loved me, and I loved it. It was brighter, hotter, and hypnotizing, kissing my cheek every morning to wake me. We've always had a love affair that kept me coming to the beach year after year. However, this morning was different. The sun didn't wake me; the pain in my body did. Ava and Lisa weren't startled by the blaring of an annoying alarm clock, but by the scream I let out due to the agony I was in at that very moment. They jumped up, rushed to my side, and helped me get out of bed. I tried to pull it together. I forced myself to shower, get dressed, and go on about my day like I wasn't just staring at death's door a few hours ago. Unfortunately, as we headed downstairs, my anxiety reared its ugly head, and decided to stay a while.

The feeling only intensified once we got outside. I started rapidly breathing, my chest tightened up, and I couldn't help looking over my shoulder because of the uncertainty of Jackson's whereabouts, especially considering law enforcement's disinterest in doing their job. I'd never had a panic attack before, but I was 100% sure I was having one. What was worse was not knowing how to make it stop. I couldn't move or take another step; it felt like I was stuck in drying cement. It became apparent to Ava and Lisa that I was struggling; I WAS NOT OK! Evidently, there was no way to salvage this weekend, so I figured it was best I went home. The girls helped me get back to the room to start packing. Since I melted down before we had a chance to eat, they decided to pick us up some food and get on the road after eating. While they were gone, I decided to lie down. When I woke up, morning had come and gone, and it was well into the evening.

Ava and Lisa were nowhere to be found. I knew they had returned from the breakfast run because my food was sitting on the table. But I wish they would have woke me up so we could head home. I thought they understood that I didn't...I couldn't be here anymore. I assumed they were downstairs in the lobby with the guys, so I called their phones but couldn't reach them. I called Trey to see if they were with them, no answer. After several attempts, over several hours, still nothing. NO ONE would answer their phone! What in the world was going on? Of all the times when I needed the phones to work, this was one of them. Myrtle Beach was infamous for phones not working during bike week, and since I was already on edge, this made it worse. I felt like I was in an episode of the Twilight Zone.

Two hours into a new day, Ava and Lisa strolled into the room, giggling and laughing. I was infuriated! I felt so disrespected...AGAIN! But this time, it was from people that I thought had my back. They completely disregarded my need to feel safe (at home with my mom) and abandoned me at my most vulnerable time. If they wanted to go off, do their thing, and be free, they should have said that. I would have been home by now. Trying to hold back my tears, I gathered my travel bag without speaking a word to either of them and left. I walked through the parking lot to my car, still praying that Jackson wasn't waiting around the building or behind a bush to finish what he started the other day. Once in the car, I threw my bags in the back seat and drove off.

The drive home was a blur. I don't remember much of it. However, I recall seeing the Winston-Salem sign and thinking, 'I can't wait to get home.' When I walked into the house, my mom was in the kitchen washing dishes. Her first words were, "What happened to you coming home yesterday?" That's not the conversation I hoped to have right off the bat, but nothing seemed to be going my way recently. I was too exhausted, physically and mentally, to go into details and reignite the anger that took me the entire drive home to shake. So I simply said, "It's not worth getting into, Mom." I dropped my keys on the table and headed down the hall to my room. All I wanted to do was shower and sleep…sleep this nightmare away.

A week passed, and I hadn't spoken about that night, and my mom never asked. I also hadn't talked to Ava and Lisa since I left them at the beach. I couldn't even tell you how they got home. My dad was having a family gathering, and I wanted to see everyone. Being around family was therapeutic and, ironically, securing for me. I exerted so much energy in keeping my abuse and attack a secret; this was my time to spend enjoying the people I love and who loved me. And it was exactly what I needed. I was one of the last to leave my dad's house. As he walked me to my car, he hesitantly asked, "So, where's Jackson?" "I don't know," I quickly responded. "We're no longer together." I thought he was going to follow that with a bunch of questions, but I was wrong. "Good, I didn't like him anyway," he said while opening the car door. "What?!" I reacted, stunned. "Dad, why are you telling me this now?" I questioned, instantly feeling angry. Rushing to explain, he says, "Well, by the time you introduced me to him, y'all had been dating a year." I leaned on the car to gather myself and looked into my father's eyes. "Daddy!" I yelled, "I don't care how long I am with someone! When I bring a man to meet you, I am seeking your approval of him; the buck stops with you!" Again, holding back the tears (it's been a lot of that recently), I took a deep breath and walked around my dad to get in the car. "Well, Baby, he's gone now, and that's all that matters," he said as he kissed me goodbye. Little did he know that his kiss was like a gut punch that I wasn't prepared for. It took the wind right out of me.

My drive back to Winston was long and hard. I cried so much I could hardly see the road. There were moments I had to pull over to get myself together for my own safety and the other drivers. I was screaming and cussing, mad at everyone and seemingly hurt by everyone, but mainly furious with myself. I questioned God why He had allowed these things to happen and wondered what I did to deserve it. Once I was all cried out, I packed up my emotions (neatly folded and tucked away) and got back on the road. During the remainder of the drive, I realized how good I was at telling myself I would be ok, although I wasn't entirely convinced. I never felt so uncertain in my life. Usually, I could think of a song that would put me into my happy place, but this time, I didn't have a song to sing me through this. I was empty.

I finally pulled into the driveway, put the car in park, and just sat in silence as the purr of the car did its best to soothe me. Suddenly, my body felt familiarly weak. In the distance, I could hear my mom calling from the door, "Victoria, you aight!?" Although I tried, I couldn't respond. I started breathing rapidly, my chest tightened up, and I felt as if someone was behind me. So, I laid my forehead on the steering wheel, closed my eyes, and whispered, Dear God...

ABOUT THE *Author*

TJ Thomas is a native of Winston-Salem, NC, but was raised in both Winston-Salem and Salisbury, NC. She is a proud member of Zeta Phi Beta Sorority, Inc., and an HBCU alumni of North Carolina Central University. TJ is, without a doubt, a proud 'Southern Country' girl through and through.

She happily resides in Powder Springs, GA, with her husband, Allan, and their Boston Terrier furbaby, Winston.

TJ has always loved writing. It has helped her release the weight of past experiences and reclaim her emotional freedom. By coming outside of her comfort zone, she has found a sense of emotional empathy and connection that has eluded her for years.

High Priced Silence, the new author's first installment of her upcoming book series, is packed with unexpected twists and turns. In writing this story, TJ was motivated by the assurance that her readers would identify with Victoria's strength amidst her personal turmoil and connect with the situations she endured in silence. Although this story isn't unique, it could only be told as

TJ could—as she, too, is a thriver and an overcomer on her path to healing.

In a personal statement, TJ reveals:

*"Healing has levels. At first, I thought my pain was just that - pain that would only heal with time. However, while I was waiting for my **WHEN**, I learned that my healing was in the **WIN**! So, I hope that somewhere between the first page and last page, my readers will also find their **WIN***